MW01265058

Best wishes to my
Friend Mary

Dave Norem

KILLING,
A *REAL-BAD*
BUSINESS

DAVE NOREM

Print ISBN: 978-1-66780-132-2

eBook ISBN: 978-1-66780-133-9

He was as dark and lean and deadly looking as a cobra.

"The gun, Mr. Real."

I slid the .45 across the floor toward the front corner and stood up, my left hand behind my back, my right hanging at my side.

He glanced over at his raised left hand, where blood was running down across his wrist and under his sleeve.

"I am going to lose my finger."

I had already noticed the pinky was dangling by a thread, so I didn't look again.

As quick as the snake that he was, his right hand dipped behind his neck and the dagger came at me like a bullet.

Anne-Marie Reynolds for Readers' Favorite

* * * * *

Killing, A Real-Bad Business by Dave Norem is a great story of retribution, a classic tale of good meets bad and real justice being served. The characters are all well-developed and the writing is descriptive enough to place you right there in the thick of it.

Enjoyed the reference to Papertown, a previous Dave Norem novel and if you've read and enjoyed that one, you'll love this one. All in all, another good, solidly written novel from a writer who has mastered the art of storytelling.

K.C. Finn for Readers' Favorite

* * * * *

Author Dave Norem has crafted a masterful action tale for fans of vengeance, thrills, and gritty realism in their characters. Norem also does a wonderful job of describing scenes and making everything so vivid. Overall, I would highly recommend Killing, A Real-Bad Business to fans of gritty action thrillers with lots of meat on their bones and for readers who like no-nonsense characters who get down to business when it counts.

If an injury has to be done to a man it should be so severe that his vengeance need not be feared.

NICOLO MACHIAVELLI

CHAPTER 1

SOME PEOPLE LIVE THEIR WHOLE LIVES WITHOUT KNOWING THEIR true calling. I've known mine since the day I turned seventeen.

I was driving my uncle's ten-year-old, 1950 A-frame wrecker down a lonely dirt road forty miles from home. Ahead of me, I saw a man at the edge of the road thumbing for a ride. Closer, I saw that it was my mom's old boyfriend. Even though I hadn't seen him in five years, I would have recognized him anywhere: the bastard who broke my nose and arm, raped my eight-year-old sister and put my mom in a coma she never came out of.

I gave him a ride all right, and a flight to go with it— on the push bumper, the hood, the roof, and briefly on top of the hoist frame. He was a tough son of a bitch; I'll give him credit for that. I was doing forty when I saw him, fifty when I hit him, and he was still alive. I had to back over him twice with the twenty-inch rear duals to finish him off.

On the way home, I thought about him and others like him. Killing him was Real-Bad business, but I knew it was meant to be.

* * *

There wasn't any significant damage to the old two-ton cab, a few scuff marks, a minor dent on the hood and a little blood that was easily wiped off. I told my uncle later I'd hit a big old buck. It wasn't too far from the truth. He'd turned and ran like one when he saw I was going to run him over.

The next day was a Sunday and early that morning I borrowed a pickup from my cousin and went back to bury him. I only had time to get him out of sight before, but now I gave him more attention. Not that it mattered, but he was named after a Canadian whiskey... Hiram Walker. I found papers on him indicating he had just been released on parole for good behavior. What a laugh! He was sent up for beating another woman to death. Well, he wouldn't be making his next meeting with his parole officer.

It turned out I was wrong about something though. I thought nobody else would miss him, but that was something I didn't find out for a long time.

There were six one-dollar bills in his cheap plastic wallet and, surprise-surprise, two fifties folded up in his watch pocket. It was more than I'd ever held at one time and I'd done the world some good as well by getting rid of him. Later on, the two fifties got more attention.

He'd rigored-up some, but all the broken bones left him limber enough. I tied his ankles to the trailer hitch and dragged him far into the woods to a good sandy spot. When I stepped out of the truck, a big, old eastern diamondback nearly bit me. Only a fast sidestep saved me. I flattened his head with the shovel and when I finished digging, I threw the snake into the hole first.

The asshole, Hiram Walker, I planted face down so he could see where he was going. His face landed on the snake, which proved to be still alive. Snakes can't dig, so I knew he wasn't going anywhere. I buried them deep and finished before noon. Occasionally I'll think back and rub two fifties together—the first two fifties I ever owned.

My name is Real-Bad, William Edward Real-Bad.

Four generations back, my great, great grandfather, a Seminole, was born with another name. He was recruited as a guide to help a posse capture or kill a gang of criminals hiding in the swamps near Okeechobee. When a deputy took him to meet the leader of the posse, his half-breed sponsor was asked, "Who's he?" Misunderstanding, and knowing they were headed into a fight, the sponsor replied, "He real bad." Great-great-grandfather proved his mettle and the name was born. Afterward, they gave him papers with the name, John Real-Bad. He and his descendents consistently married whites.

CHAPTER 2

Two years later, I was in France with one year of service under my belt. The Army, in its infinite wisdom, sent me to intelligence school. It wasn't what I wanted but there were still plenty of opportunities to learn the physical stuff too. A man planning to work outside the law could benefit by learning the intelligence business as well. I took advantage of the gyms and martial arts classes and volunteered for every seminar involving weapons and hand-to-hand combat. They must have figured me for a career man, because they allowed me plenty of training in both.

I was also fortunate enough to become friends with some Army Rangers, damn good men who take care of bad business for all of us.

Intelligence training was interesting enough but the actual work afterward was mostly boring, even in western France. Duties varied from reading English-language newspapers and magazines for dissention against the good old US, to observing and scanning crowds at political rallies for repeat faces. We also watched border crossings from Germany and spied on our own officers and their families. The last of these led to some interesting affiliations, not always the kind my superiors wanted or knew about. I have my own sense of fair play.

At the end of my first year's service in 1962, I went home to Florida on leave. Someone was waiting for me when I stepped down from the bus, a stranger. He was in his mid-thirties, clean shaven and about my size. The man stepped forward, "Mr. Real-Bad?"

I looked him over good before answering. He was dressed neat, wearing tan, low-heeled western boots and a matching vest that partially concealed a shoulder-holstered pistol. His jeans were pressed to a sharp crease and under the vest he wore a long-sleeved, solid-blue polo shirt. A cream-colored western hat topped it off. His clothes fit together well without looking gaudy or out of place. His face was sun weathered, but not tanned to leather. I thought he might have been Army CID. He had a military look to him, but not the manner. I was stumped.

I nodded my head in acknowledgement and he stepped forward with his hand outstretched for a shake. "Jerry Smith, I've been looking forward to meeting you."

"For what purpose?"

He motioned to the side. "Can we sit down over here on the bench?"

I thought, this can't be good.

As we sat down, he turned back the right side of his vest and showed me a badge pinned to the lining. He said, "William, I'm a US Marshal and I'm only looking for information."

"Go ahead."

"Do you remember a man named Hiram Walker?"

I took a couple seconds to think that one over. I'm sure my surprise was evident. "I'm not likely to forget that son of a bitch. Did he break out?"

"No. He was released and then disappeared."

"Should we be worried? Is he coming after us? I did testify against him."

"No, I don't think so. He disappeared almost two years ago."

"How could he have been released? He killed at least two women and raped God knows how many women and kids."

"I'm sorry, the US Marshal's Service had nothing to do with that. We only became involved because he disappeared. But we need to get back to my question."

I shut up, but he could tell I wasn't happy about it.

"Have you seen him, or did you see him two years ago—before you went in service?"

"No! I probably would have put a bullet into him as an escapee if I had."

"Oh, I'm not accusing you of anything. I know you were in the area he disappeared from at the time. I have to ask these questions."

He was hitting too close to home. "Whoa! There's more too this than you're telling me."

"You are sure you never saw him?"

"No, I never saw him!"

"OK, here's what happened. US Customs had him released. He had connections with smugglers and vowed to turn against them for a reduced sentence. After he led them into a trap, he was to go back to prison and serve another two years—still a big reduction. But he vanished like smoke."

"Shit."

"They initially didn't want to admit they lost him, let alone the five hundred dollars they fronted him. Then they tried following his movements themselves. By the time I acquired the information and tracked him as far as I could, you were already gone."

I figured the five hundred dollars amount might be a little trap to see if I would mention a different number. I hadn't forgotten the two fifties and I didn't fall for it.

"He probably skipped with the money, or maybe the smugglers did him in and kept it. What does all this have to do with me?"

"Probably nothing, but we know he was last seen around Starke, heading south on foot. On the same day, you were driving from Orange Park to Ocala."

"What makes you think that?"

"You dropped off a wrecked car in Orange Park and went back to Ocala. Coincidence?"

"Yes, I remember the return trip. I went down through the National Forest on my way back. If he was there, I never saw him." That wasn't close to where I'd run over him.

"OK William, I have to ask."

We sat there for a couple minutes in silence before he said, "How's the Army treating you?"

"Good so far. I don't know yet where I'll wind up or how long I'll stay. Were you in?"

"Yes, I planned to make a career of it, but Korea changed my mind. Nothing that happens here is as bad as we had it over there. Now there's another war brewing, Vietnam, and I don't want any part of it. Avoid it if you can."

He seemed satisfied with my answers, or at least he knew he wouldn't get any more out of me, and we parted company. I had a feeling I hadn't seen the last of US Marshal Jerry Smith. Up until then, I had no idea someone was tracking Hiram Walker and that it would lead back to me. Before I heard any more about it, I was gone.

* * *

Shortly after returning to France, my second order of real-bad business tested my recently gained skills. While stationed in France we sometimes worked and stayed on the other side of the border in Stuttgart. Stuttgart was a booming industrial city with a plethora of foreign nationals. Ethnic areas were scattered around the city's perimeter, separating the different nationalities from the mainstream German population. Two nationalities of particular interest to us were Turkish and Greek.

It was in one of these areas a friend, Robert Cee, and I were visiting a no-name gasthaus with a recessed entryway. Two Americans were standing at the bar, but we didn't know them. There were many American military personnel in the area, most of them wearing civilian clothes when out on the town, and we blended in well. Tensions seemed to run high in this particular place though, and we were observing.

I was sitting on an extended bench along the front wall and Robert was sitting to my left with his back to the entry divider. The rectangular table ran perpendicular to the front of the building, so I was at one end. Chairs positioned around the exposed sides of it and the other tables complemented the remaining seats in the house.

From the entrance on the left, a mahogany stand-up bar with a brass foot rail extended to the far wall. Across from us, a jukebox sat next to an open doorway into a short hall leading to restrooms in both directions—Herren on the left, where men pissed on the wall and let it run down into a gutter, and Damen on the right, where women sat on regular toilets and gazed at the hair on their legs. I once had the misfortune of entering the wrong one in a similar place and knew the stalls would have no doors.

The other seats at our table were closer to the door and had an ebb and flow of Europeans of both sexes.

Several tough looking, middle-aged Turks with huge moustaches and craggy features surrounded the table to our right. With them were three younger-looking German women wearing knee-length dresses. Two tables over, several Greeks caught my attention, as they were typically enemies of the Turks. I saw occasional, furtive, hostile glances both ways. In between was a table of all German men, most in their thirties. Other tables were surrounded with a mix of middle-aged nationalities of both sexes.

This place was a powder keg waiting to explode and we had picked our spots early so we could keep an eye on everyone and not get caught up in the eruption.

The action started when one of the Americans from the bar went to the jukebox and stood there trying to interpret the selections. One of the German girls from the next table quickly rose and walked over to the jukebox where she leaned against the American. It was apparent they knew each other and she was soliciting him to let her select the music. He put his arm around her waist and she didn't resist.

He was tall, skinny and young with light brown hair and prominent cheekbones. She was short with dark hair in a pixie haircut and an impish face. Her blue eyes and milk-white skin contrasted the black hair on her arms and head. She was also four or five years older than the American. This girl had been getting her kicks for a while and didn't mind playing both ends against the middle.

Next to her chair, sitting on the far side of the table facing us, was the meanest looking of the Turks. He was around six feet tall, forty years old and hawk-nosed with a long horizontal scar on his right cheek. He jumped to his feet so fast his chair fell over backward against one of the Germans. Ignoring the chair, the Turk lunged toward the girl at the jukebox.

She looked over her shoulder to the right, at the change in sound, just in time to catch his open left hand with the back of her head. The blow knocked her to the side and against the doorframe. Before she could fall or regain her balance, he landed a solid blow between her shoulder blades with his fist. It knocked her through the doorway and against the divider wall, where she fell to her hands and knees. He followed up with solid kicks from behind, pacing her as she crawled into the restroom.

The Turk had barely missed the young American with the first blow, and he may have intended to hit him as well. Stunned, the American was still standing at the jukebox with his jaw somewhere down around his navel.

Not everyone was so slow. Robert started to rise before the Turk had even cleared his table, but I grabbed his arm and yanked him back down. There was no way of knowing which way this wind was going to blow. We needed to keep a low profile.

Everyone but us leaped to their feet. The Turk's friends were quickest. They overwhelmed their compatriot with sheer numbers and dragged him back to his seat. I anticipated a major brawl but Ingrid, the owner, raced to center-floor imploring them all to remain seated in several languages, promising free beer.

KILLING, A REAL-BAD BUSINESS

Ingrid was tall, slender and shapely, with long black hair twisted, tied and piled on top of her head. She appeared to be in her early-to-mid thirties, but she was also a woman who would remain ageless—and always attractive. She surprised us with her commanding presence of mind and use of languages, but that was what we were looking for. She was a main source of false documents and a gateway for terrorists. This little gasthaus didn't survive on beer and brotchen alone.

Everyone sat and things calmed with a collective sigh. The German girl and one of her friends still hadn't come out of the restroom. The young American who'd been at the jukebox glared at the Turk and shook his fist as if he could conquer the world. The Turk pulled something from inside his shirt and held it aloft toward the American's face. It took me a moment, but I was still way ahead of the young soldier at the bar.

The Turk was flaunting a cord strung with at least half-a-dozen human ears, some withered and blackened and some not so old. It sunk in, and the boy turned back toward the bar and gripped the rail, the way his pal had been doing from the start. They left shortly thereafter and we followed them out. They looked back at us, first in fear and then in obvious relief. The shorter friend started to speak.

I cut him off. "Get the fuck out of here and don't come back." His mouth clamped shut as I stepped toward them and raised my voice. "Move!"

They moved—from the tone of my voice if nothing else. I had grown some and put on muscle during the past three years, gaining a few scars from training partners and from personal experience along the way. Despite the changes, I could have passed for a banker, minister or insurance agent with my straight, brown hair, blue eyes and bland features. At six-foot, 190, I still possessed a full set of teeth and the scars weren't noticeable unless you looked closely.

Robert cursed under his breath. "That Turk son of a bitch, I wanted to kill him right on the spot. We know he's been killing Americans all over Europe. You know about the torture and missing ears as well as I do!"

"It's not our fight man, and not why we're here either. It's the woman we were told to locate." We had seen the Turk before, more than once while surveying crowds, but I hadn't wanted to get Robert inflamed by mentioning it.

Robert knew, he still needed to vent a little. He was taller than me by three inches, but was only a few pounds heavier. His blue-black hair, and the heavy beard he couldn't quite shave off, made him look like a gangly Jewish schoolteacher with big hands and feet. But the looks were deceiving. He was fast and accurate with both fists and feet. The long arms and legs hit and kicked damned hard.

While most of the men we'd trained with were content to look hard and live soft, with dreams of an office in Washington, Robert and I were on common ground.

As we walked along, I asked, "Do you want to get him?"

"You mean the Turk with the scar?"

"Right, who else?"

He laughed, "Damn right—I want him."

I grabbed his arm and stopped him so we were facing. "You know we'd have to kill him… and maybe some of the others too." Our eyes locked.

This particular Turk was one we were looking for off the record. Young Americans, both male and female, civilian and military, were tortured, killed and mutilated in areas near the border. We had spotted him in more than one of those areas. He was an equal opportunity butcher.

Robert held my stare and hesitated only a moment, serious now. "Yeah, I can do it."

I already knew I could. And I would. Robert seemed to know it too and we continued on our way without further discussion.

CHAPTER 3

IT TOOK US ALMOST TWO WEEKS TO SET IT UP. WE WENT UP TO METZ, far from our usual travels, and recruited a little French whore named Clair, along with her pimp-brother Didier. Both were blonde and blue-eyed with delicate features.

They crossed the German border illegally, stuffed into the trunk of the old Citroen DS19 that Robert was driving. The car crawled away from stops, smoked, and sounded like a popcorn popper. On the plus side, it was roomy and provided a soft, cushiony ride. Once rolling, it would go fast and hold the road like it was on rails.

We had already paid the siblings half the money, twice as much as they would have made in a night, and we let Didier stash the money away in their apartment while Clair waited with us. They convinced themselves we were CIA agents bent on interrogating a spy. We let them believe what they wanted.

Once we knew our man was there and seats at the bar were still empty, we sent the two into the gasthaus to stand at the bar. They were to get the Turk into the car, which was parked in a dark alley a block away, stall the engine, and then run away from it. We would pick them up two hours later at the Bahnhoff. We rigged the car so it would stall on its own in case they decided to ditch us or something else went wrong. A solenoid valve in the fuel line, and a hidden switch, did the trick.

It didn't take long for the petite little blonde to entice the Turk into following them out of the gasthaus. She fawned on him and explained in her broken German that her brother owned an auto and would take them to her apartment. Once there, they would both have the pleasure of servicing him.

We anticipated that most likely some of the Turk's compatriots would follow him for backup, and maybe as many as four or five of them. We would just have to deal with it. Earlier we raided a construction site and swiped several steel, meter-long pieces of concrete reinforcement rod. We picked hiding places for ourselves and stashed the rods in several locations in the alley.

Before the three of them entered the alley, Robert boosted me up to crawl into a higher-level, recessed window opening and hid himself in a doorway beyond where we expected the car to stall. We had no illusions about the Turks. Whether it was just the one, or several, they would try to kill us. We weren't sure about guns but they would certainly have knives and brass knuckles or batons, all of which were plentiful in the area.

We weren't wrong. Five of them followed half-a-block behind, three abreast followed by two. As soon as the blondes and the Turk with the scar were all in the car, the rest of them rushed toward it, passing me as they went. There was no time to waste and I dropped into the alley behind them. Robert was too far away and I was overtaking the five Turks without him.

As I came up behind them, Didier started the car and accelerated down the alley. One of the two I was coming up on must have heard my shoe squeak on the cobblestones. He spun toward me, and his partner followed suit. It flashed through my mind that I didn't want to kill them, but I struck hard anyway as he was turning. The steel bar came down past his right ear and impacted his neck, shoulder and collar bone. I heard something snap.

He was down but not out and I stepped back momentarily, forcing his partner to leap over him to get at me. My bar caught him in the ribs in mid air and he hit the ground doubled up on his side. I kicked him between the eyes and kept going, leaping over both of them. A third one was at me from the left and I brought the bar straight down onto his right arm with a satisfying crunch and heard metal clatter to the stones. The others were at me as well and I kept swinging my steel bar. They seemed to keep popping back up after I knocked them down. There were yells, grunts, and curses. Some of them may have been mine.

Something snagged my sleeve and I felt a sting on my right arm. I grabbed an arm with my left hand, raised it high, and kicked at the matching leg. He went down. I saw another arm raise and I jabbed the end of my rebar straight in under it, going for the armpit. Then I was down.

I rolled to avoid kicks and stabs while still swinging the bar and connecting with legs. Then all motion stopped with a thud. There was only one man standing, and it was Robert. He reached down for me and said, "Come on!"

I scrambled to my feet and tried to catch up with him as he raced toward the back of the car.

Didier had passed Robert's hiding place before the car stalled. He bailed out without waiting to see if his sister made it.

She didn't.

The man was sitting on the back seat with the girl as we approached from behind. Robert smacked the window on her side with his open palm. I yanked the door open on the other side. The Turk had a solid grip on the back of her neck with his left hand. His right held the point of a dagger between her lips, and at least two inches into her mouth.

I shot him in the knee with the six-millimeter Pic revolver I'd brought for the occasion. He was a tough, experienced killer but he couldn't stop himself from shrieking and grabbing at his knee. He yanked his dagger out of her mouth in the process.

With the strength of someone twice her size, she punched him in the balls and wrenched free, leaving him to us.

We didn't waste much time on him in the Silberwald Forest Park. We'd already taken his wallet, passport, and two more knives from him by the time we had him well away from the car and on the ground. Robert kicked his injured knee and put the barrel of my pistol against the Turk's eye. I pushed the point of the dagger into his mouth the way he'd done Clair. The only difference was, I kept right on pushing.

He put up a hell of a struggle, but it wasn't enough. We left him naked and dead without any documents—his string of ears crammed into his bloody mouth, his own ears among them.

On the way back to the car, I discovered I was cut on the arm, although it was superficial. There was a lump on the side of my head too. I wondered aloud if any of the others were dead.

"Man that was something," Robert said. "You had them all, even when you were on the ground. You were about to knee-cap the last one with your rod when I conked him. They're not dead but at least two are fucked up for life."

* * *

We had pitched the steel bars after we left the park and the pistol went down a sewer drain on a city street.

We gave Clair and Didier the Turk's money, along with the other half we'd promised. After we delivered them back into France, Didier commented, "Murder should pay better."

I countered with, "We would be money ahead with a triple murder."

Clair smacked his face, and in her broken English, said, "Fool, we never see murder, and he need to be kill."

A month later, I wound up back in Stuttgart.

CHAPTER 4

HALFWAY THROUGH MY FIVE-MILE RUN WITH FULL GEAR, A JEEP WAS waiting at the top of a hill. My platoon sergeant said, "Get in. You are ordered to the CO's office... on the double". It was fall, 1962, nine months since the encounter with the Turks, so that wasn't it. During the interim, I had made some new enemies by getting the goods on a Full Colonel named Boris Rathke for arms smuggling. Rathke had friends. I could only think, oh shit.

Colonel Plender didn't like me and I didn't like him. It pissed him off whenever he saw my hyphenated last name in black letters fronting a white background on my fatigue shirt. Fortunately, most of the time we wore civilian clothes while on assignment.

He handed me an envelope. "Change into full civilian, Bad." He refused to say my full name. "And get your ass over to Stuttgart. Markham will drive you. After you get there, not before, open this, read it, memorize it and then burn it. Dismissed."

We went straight to the airfield where an L 19 fixed-wing was waiting with the engine running. The propeller backwash nearly blew my hat off before I clamped it down onto my head as I approached from the rear. That model plane was called a Bird Dog and there's only room for two in it, one behind the other, pilot in front. I was crammed in behind a pilot I never even got a good look at and the noise was too deafening to talk. Before I could even get my shoulder and lap belts fastened, we were rolling down the runway.

The hand-printed letter told me I was to pick up a defector and escort him through several flights, back to Stuttgart: brief and to the point, only need-to-know information. The flight crews each had their own set of orders and knew where and when.

As soon as I was out of the plane, a GI was waiting to grab my arm. He was wearing standard green Army fatigues, no hat, and without name or rank. "Real-Bad?" I nodded and he said. "I'm George. Come on." He led me across the PSP to where an old CH 34 cargo helicopter was waiting, already blasting us with dirt. I climbed over the dropped-down seat, through the cargo door, and sat on the bench on the opposite side. A Spec. 5 sat on the same bench on my left, below the copilot's seat, wearing a flight helmet plugged into the system intercom. He glanced over but only nodded at me. George followed me in and pulled the seat-step up, latched it, and slid the door closed.

He grinned as he looked across at me, then sat down on my right and held out his hand, and we shook. "George Rickson. I don't know much more than you do. We are going to drop down across the border and pick up a passenger. If he needs help, you are it. None of the rest of us can leave this thing."

I just nodded. It was hard to talk with all of the noise. George glanced up over the door, and I noticed a long rifle strapped above it, not one of ours, it was a Russian Mosin-Nagent with open sights, probably chambered in 7.62mm. They were usually scope-mounted and used as sniper rifles.

"I'm the only one here that's armed," he said. I gave him a thumbs-up in acknowledgement.

After fifteen minutes, the helicopter sat down in a hay field, but the pilot kept the rotors turning. George went back into the tail section and returned with two rolls of green tape. It was an all-purpose Army tape and I wasn't sure what he had in mind. "Come on, you can help," he yelled across at me as he jumped out. He started taping over the aircraft numbers. I caught on and pitched in. He hollered, "The U.S. Army too."

We loaded back up and continued on for another twenty or thirty minutes, changing course several times. Then, George got a hand signal from the crew chief. He stepped across and opened the sliding cargo door. I saw the fences below us. There were six or seven in parallel, and another set of posts, each fence about twenty yards apart, across the rolling hills. They were a hodgepodge of barbed wire and concertina wire.

We stayed on our side of the wire for a short ways before the man appeared in a dip between two hills. He was running for all he was worth toward the fences, wearing clothes far too bulky for the endeavor. Only two rises beyond him, several others, in drab, brownish-gray uniforms, were also running in the same direction.

"Get ready," George hollered as he unstrapped the rifle. The helicopter dropped closer to the ground, placing us out of sight of the soldiers. Without waiting, the pilot slid the craft sideways, dropped and hovered only a couple feet above the ground, just beyond the last set of posts. George moved to the front of the opening and unlatched the seat. It swung outward from a hinged base and the bottom of it became a step.

George braced himself against the doorframe with the rifle extended. "I'll keep them off your back."

I didn't stick around long enough to answer. When we were within forty yards of the man, the pilot set the helicopter down but kept the engine at a high RPM, rotors flattened out. I could tell the man we were after was exhausted as I jumped out and raced to meet him.

He was in his forties or fifties and unshaven, with shaggy black hair and wire-framed glasses. As I grabbed an arm to speed things up, I noticed one lens was missing from his glasses. The arm I grabbed was as thin as a stick under three or four layers of clothes.

Above us, George was firing the Mosin-Nagent, working the bolt like a pro. The two of us made it to the flipped-down seat-step and my man collapsed onto it. I had to grab him by the collar and one pants leg to boost him on up. The crew chief grabbed his arm and dragged him on in. I almost made it.

CHAPTER 5

HALFWAY INTO THE HELICOPTER, I HEARD TWO LOUD BANGS, LIKE A large tablespoon hitting the bottom of a metal wash pan, hard. A moment later, a sledgehammer hit me in the small of the back. My legs collapsed and I lost my grip with one hand. The CH 34 was already lifting off. Half in shock, I held onto the seat frame in desperation.

A strong hand grabbed my free wrist, and another grabbed my collar. As I landed on the deck, I stupidly yelled, "I've been shot!"

George grinned down at me with the whitest teeth I'd ever seen on a man. You think and say the damnedest things when your central nervous system takes a hit.

"You'll live," he hollered back as he hoisted the seat back into the hold and slammed the door shut. I heard one more bang before it closed completely. By then we were up and away and I noticed my man reclining on the floor on the other side, propped against the seat and still wheezing, staring at me. He never said a word. The crew chief had already strapped himself back in and was talking into his microphone, but I couldn't hear the words above the roar of the engine and the pounding of the rotors.

I tried to sit up but my legs wouldn't work. I had no feeling down there. George reached down, unbuckled my belt, and unzipped my pants. Everything seemed to be in slow motion with jerky moves from one thing to the next. Before I could comprehend what he was doing, he rolled me over onto my belly and yanked my pants down to my knees: my undershorts too. I heard him curse under his breath and say something else, but the engine roared louder and I couldn't make out what he said.

He pushed my shirt and undershirt up with one hand and I could feel him pushing or pulling on my lower back. Then he pulled something loose and a sharp, jagged pain shot through me from my spine into my guts. I gritted my teeth to keep from screaming.

On his knees, George leaned over again and spoke right into my ear. "Like I said, you'll live!" He held a spent, bloody bullet between his finger and thumb. He put it into his pants pocket and began opening a first aid kit. Before I knew it, and while the initial pain was subsiding, he pulled out a packaged syringe. He quickly swabbed my exposed butt cheek and drove the needle home.

After putting a field dressing on my back and taping it down with considerable force, and then topping it with more green tape, he pulled my shirt down and rolled me back over. I grabbed my own undershorts and pulled them up but let him finish the job. I was too spent to care. The crew chief, a Spec 5 named Norem, ignored us during all of this, while my man watched everything we did, as if he was memorizing it.

George went back toward the tail section and returned with two blankets. He handed one to the man and then spread the other one over me. He finished by tucking it in around me; quite a thoughtful fellow. I was watching him like the other man was watching both of us. George was a good-looking man, about my age, with dark-brown, wavy hair, slightly long by Army standards. He had broad shoulders and strong looking hands. He was busy strapping the rifle back above the cargo door while I looked him over. Then, despite my efforts to stay awake, I fell asleep just as my back began to throb.

* * *

When I awoke, I had no idea where I was or how I got there. I could tell I was in a military hospital though. I was flat on my back in a bed, strapped down, but not cuffed. The twenty-four-hour clock on the wall showed 09:30. The door was closed and there was no one else in the room with me. I closed my eyes and tried to replay it in my mind, starting with Plender's office. And then it started coming back—the mission, the one I failed to complete.

Shortly, a nurse arrived in a strange uniform, and only a minute later, a graying Air Force major in his forties came in. The nurse had only given me a fleeting smile before she began checking hoses and the IV bag.

"Where am I?"

The major answered, "Frankfort Air Force Base."

"How did I get up here? How long have I been here?"

"You arrived some time last night. How are you feeling?"

"Like I've been run over by a truck, and groggy."

"Can you move your feet?

I was surprised to find out I could. He had me raise each leg, extended. I could, but it made me break into a sweat from the effort.

Bending my knees, twisting my ankles and wiggling my toes were much easier.

He told me to roll onto my side, and with the nurse helping, he ripped the tape loose from my back. The pain from pulling it free was minor compared to the jolt I got in my spine. "Ah, you will be just fine in a couple days."

"How deep is the bullet hole?"

"Bullet hole? Is that what happened? It just looks like you've been hit with the back side of a claw hammer."

"You didn't know?"

He smiled with gray teeth that matched his hair and I could smell pipe smoke on his breath. "Son, I don't have a need to know."

He watched as the nurse applied a new bandage. For the first time, she spoke. "I am taping this one on diagonally." Then to me, "The one we just removed was taped vertically. A previous one was taped horizontally." The major nodded. They lowered me to my back again and he patted me on the leg. They left without saying anything more.

The next morning, at about the same time, there was a light knock on the door before it swung open. George Rickson walked in with his bright-white grin. "How you feeling, Soldier?"

"Fine, and how did you get here?" I held out my hand. "My friends call me Will."

He pulled up a chair as we shook. "I'm on special assignment, Will, and you are part of it. See, I owe you an apology. I was supposed to protect you by shooting near enough to them to scare them off."

"You didn't shoot any of them?"

"No. I came close, real close. Just between us, my orders were not to shoot them, just shoot close enough to drive them back. I parted their hair, they just didn't scare. Maybe they were more afraid of the consequences of letting him get away. If you hadn't made it, we would have had to leave you."

I had the feeling his orders were to finish me off if I didn't make it. But I didn't say so. What-ifs and would-haves don't buy anything. It didn't matter what he would have done. Maybe he didn't know himself. Instead, I said, "Well, you saved my life anyway."

"Part of the job, Will. I delivered your man and someone else brought you here, all hush-hush. The job is not finished until we get you back to France." He handed me the bullet, only slightly deformed. "Cheap commie ammo is what saved you. Not enough powder to do the job. They only put one hole and a dent in the helicopter. When we stopped to pull off the green tape, I rammed a stick through the bullet hole so it looked like we flew into a tree. That's for the pilot to explain, not us."

"Interesting occupation you have, George."

"I'll have to say the same about you."

What went unsaid was what he would have done if I hadn't made it to the helicopter. Would he have shot me? Them? Or both? I could only give him the benefit of the doubt. I never did find out anything about the man we picked up, or why we went after him at such risk in the first place.

George and I both laughed and then we talked about other things. He grew up in Indiana. I grew up in Florida. He joined with the idea of being an auto mechanic and went to school for it, but they found out he could shoot. I wanted to be a machinist, but they told me my talents would be wasted. That was the Army way. We agreed to stay in touch and exchanged contact information. I had a strong feeling we would be seeing each other again.

When I reported back to Colonel Plender a few days later, he asked me, "Did you complete your assignment?"

"The assignment was completed."

"How do you know it was completed? I heard there was a problem."

This jackass knew what happened all along. He just wanted to bust my balls. "There was a minor problem. I was shot."

"Well, we can hardly give you a medal, or a Purple Heart, for getting shot in the back, can we? Think of the implications."

I didn't bother to answer. I just wanted to get out of there. I was still having pains in my back and needles and pins in my feet and toes. It moved around.

"Actually, you did good——Bad." Then he laughed like a hyena. "I am going to give you something though. I'm giving you thirty days bereavement and personal affairs leave. Go back to the States and enjoy your time off."

"Thank you sir."

"Dismissed."

CHAPTER 6

THE THIRTY DAYS OFF HELPED. I WENT BACK TO FLORIDA AND STAYED with my uncle while I tracked down friends from high school. The pain in my back eased, but I still had intermittent pains and numbness in my left leg.

A friend, Larry, invited me to a Fourth-of-July boating party out on the edge of the Gulf, in Crystal Bay. I was odd-man-out as we motored out into the bay to rendezvous with three other boats. Larry and Pete, another high school friend brought girlfriends with them. The girls were cute, but shapeless in a teeny-bopper way in their two-piece swim suits. They were two or three years younger than me and probably still in school. I didn't remember seeing them before.

We lashed the four boats loosely together, bow-to-bow, in a plus configuration. The water was warm and only chest deep and the sun felt good. My wound had closed but it was still red and tender, so I wore a wife-beater undershirt with my trunks. No one questioned my wearing the shirt, so I didn't have to come up with an excuse.

The people in the other three boats were all couples too, with one exception, and I didn't know any of them. The exception was a sister to one of the guys and she was about my age. She was very pretty and as we milled around in the water, hopping from boat to boat, I worked my way closer.

I introduced myself and she told me her name was Eva. Short, curly black hair framed a fine-featured face above a slender, shapely body. A natural tan complexion and light-brown eyes gave her a Nefertiti look. Eva was friendly but she kept a slight distance between us and she had a faraway look in her eyes. I tried to draw her out but she wouldn't talk about herself.

"Are you in the military?" she asked.

"Yes, I'm in the Army and I'm home on a thirty-day leave."

"Have you been to Vietnam?"

"No, I'm stationed in France, and sometimes Germany."

"Oh, I'll bet Europe is nice."

Before I could answer, she turned and swam away, so I elected to let her have her space. Her short, tight curls and fine features drew me in, but as she turned, her left hand came to the surface and I saw a wedding ring.

I continued working my way around the boats. Everyone else was boat hopping and trying each other's beer and wine. I was already used to European beer and didn't get the buzz the rest of them seemed to be feeling. Still, it was a good time and a relief from the stress of what I had been doing.

Swimming was good for my back, but it was getting sore, so I hoisted myself up into Larry's boat. Everyone else seemed to be clustered around the one opposite so I enjoyed a few minutes of solitude. I was sitting in the stern, gazing out over the bay, when the water swirled practically under my nose. Then a head popped up. I thought at first it might be a dolphin, because they do that, even in shallow water.

Eight fingers gripped the transom, then Eva looked straight up at me. "I will talk to you, but not now, not here."

"OK."

"Where are you staying?"

"With my bachelor uncle near Ocala."

"What's the address, Dummy?"

I laughed and gave her the address.

She only said one more word. "Tomorrow," before she sank out of sight.

* * *

The following afternoon, my uncle and I had just gone into the house for a beer after pulling the transmission from an old Ford pickup. We heard a horn and since he was the only one standing, he looked out the window. "Do you know a woman with a blue and white Ford?"

"Maybe." I had forgotten about Eva, but that's who it was. I walked on out to the car where she sat behind the steering wheel, nervously drumming the fingers of one hand on the top of it.

I leaned down to the window and gave her a good, close look. Her left arm was on the armrest and I couldn't tell if the ring was still there. She was wearing a white print dress with little black flowers on it. It ended halfway up her thighs. "Eva!"

"I can only stay a minute. If you drive up Route 19 by Fanning, there's a bargain store on the left."

"I know it."

"Meet me there at 8:00."

"OK Eva, I'll be there." I knew we wouldn't be shopping. The store closed at 7:00.

She reached over with her right hand and tapped me on the forearm with her fingers, just once, put her Ford in reverse and backed away. There wasn't time for me to say anything. It was the first time we touched, and the touch lingered.

I mentally cursed myself. Life has enough problems without getting involved with a married woman. It just didn't sit right with me. I would just have to tell her how I felt and try not to hurt her feelings while doing it. Women are so damn difficult. Damn it!

My uncle didn't even ask when I came back in. He just rubbed his bald head and continued looking for food.

* * *

The Ford sat alone in the back corner of the parking lot. I was driving the old forty-nine Plymouth two-door sedan I owned before joining the Army. I saw no point in buying anything newer until I settled down. I arrived right on the dot so she wouldn't have to wait. For her to sit there alone wasn't a good idea anyway. There were too many crazies running up and down US 19.

She was parked facing the highway and I nosed in beside her so we were sitting face-to-face.

"We can't stay here, Will. Do you mind leaving your car and riding with me?"

I backed around her in a U-turn and parked facing out on her passenger side, then stepped over into her car. She took off almost before I got the door closed.

"You probably think I'm crazy."

"No, I think you are married."

"Not exactly."

"You'll have to explain that one to me. Either you're married or you aren't."

"In that case, I'm not." she said as she worked her way through the gears.

She drove on while I chewed on what she told me, not forgetting the ring. It was now conspicuous by its absence. I gazed out the window. I thought it best not to look at her, especially her legs.

Then she spoke again, and swiped at her eye. "I have been a widow for three months. We were only married for three weeks when they sent him to Vietnam. He was only over there for two months when he was killed."

I reached over and let my hand rest on her shoulder. "I'm sorry."

She drove on in silence traveling east. Gainesville came and went and we were heading into familiar territory. I gave her shoulder a little squeeze and then reached down and patted her thigh. She flinched at first but didn't say anything.

"I hope I don't look like him."

"No you don't, and that's a good thing. I don't want to be seen with another man yet. It's too soon. People wouldn't understand. I just want to put that part of my life aside for a while.

She turned off the state highway and started driving slow on the back roads. Ironically, we were getting close to where I had last seen Hiram Walker and it was getting dark. Wouldn't that be the joker in the deck. A fire lane opened up on one side and she eased into it. When she stopped, I advised her to go farther and turn the car around. If another car came along, we could turn the lights on and they wouldn't be able to see us inside the car.

We switched seats, and I did the backing and turning for her while she watched out the back window. Neither one of us wanted to step out in snake country. When we had switched places, she slid across my lap in a lightning move, but it was still electric.

Once I shut off the ignition, the silence came swooping in on us. Then the peeper frogs and night birds started their chorus, loud enough to hear through the closed windows. It was hot, but we had to keep the mosquitoes at bay. The Ford had a big bench seat and I moved it back as far as it would go, before sliding over to the middle.

"Just hold me please."

I hugged her for quite a while, holding her until she stopped trembling. Afterward, I gently kissed her face, hands and arms without making a move toward her breasts or legs.

Finally, we kissed. Slowly and softly at first, and then she came alive. In another minute we were both so hot it was like a wrestling match, twisting, pulling, caressing, grasping, panting. She rose on top of me and pulled the dress over her head in a single move.

I reached up and turned on the dome light for a better look. She had her hands behind her unfastening her skimpy brassiere. She wasn't wearing any panties. The hair I was gazing at was as thick and curly as the hair on her head.

She flung the brassiere into the back where the dress wound up a moment before. Then she reached up and turned off the light.

"God, you're beautiful," I moaned. I wanted to taste every inch of her.

"Do you have a condom? I quit the pill two months ago." She was already trying to get my pants down.

"No!" I gasped.

"Then you'll have to pull out!"

I grabbed her shoulders and rolled her underneath. "I can't do that with you on top."

The Ford had a long, wide seat and we used every inch of it. We even blew the horn a couple times with our feet.

We stayed there until the wee hours, the humidity overwhelming and the windows completely fogged over. Smart girl, she had brought two beach towels and two damp washcloths in a jar. Between us, we drank a gallon of iced tea.

Eventually we both had to pee so bad we couldn't wait any longer. I went out first and thrashed around in the brush for a while to scare off whatever snakes lay in wait, and then peed, while she held her foot on the brake for light. I thrashed around some more and returned to the car, where I held the brake for her.

She wouldn't give me a phone number, an address, or a planned date. I never knew when she would show up, but we met four more times before my leave was over. I tried to get her to go to a motel, but she wouldn't have it. From then on, I was better prepared, but it was still making love in the car. It was a good thing she had a vinyl seat cover. We nearly wore it out.

When I told her I had to report back, she kissed me fiercely, holding me by the ears. Without relinquishing her grip, she said, "Will, I don't want to worry about another man in the military. I want to put you out of my mind, even though I know I can't. I need to be married, so let's just go our separate ways and move on with our lives."

I could only nod and kiss her through her tears.

After I left I wondered if she had been telling me the truth or if she really was married. I could probably ask my friend, Larry to find out. But then I decided I didn't want to know.

CHAPTER 7

WHEN I RETURNED TO FRANCE, COLONEL PLENDER WAS GONE AND I had a TDY assignment to Manila, Philippines; more boring observations.

Off duty, I toured the city in a cab I hired for the day. We were stopped in traffic when I noticed a small Filipino man on the sidewalk, turning with his back to a wall. The man appeared to be in his forties and was under attack by three larger and younger men in an apparent attempt to rob him. In moments, one of them ran away screaming with his hands held to his face, another lay moaning on the sidewalk with an obviously broken elbow, and the third lay unconscious or dead. I exited the cab to ask the man how he did it.

The older man squared off facing me. "No, I am a friend," I stated as I held my hands up, palms facing outward. For emphasis, I kicked the man with the broken elbow in the head, silencing him. Then I heard sirens.

"Come on, I said, Police! Get in the cab with me. He hesitated for a moment, then nodded and relaxed his stance. The cab rolled away with police running by on both sides. The older man was crouched on the floor in the back, under my knees. The police only glanced at me as they passed. Later, a friend told me the one who ran away lost an eye. The unconscious one laying on the sidewalk had his temple punctured by a house key driven at high force by the older man's hand. Dead or alive was unknown. The one with the broken elbow would recover.

From this man, Nico Antonio, I learned about Silat fighting.

CHAPTER 8

George

GEORGE RICKSON WAS FED UP WITH THE CIA, AND THE ARMY TOO for that matter. He would wait around for long periods with nothing serious to do. He worked on fitness, hand-to-hand combat and shooting exercises in his spare time. Nothing to do was punctuated by mundane shit details such as guard duty, garbage truck driver and courier or driver for any visiting officers.

Then his contact-agent would send him off somewhere to kill someone. After Basic and Sniper training, George spent the next eleven months in Vietnam. When his agent transferred to Germany, George moved there too. They kept him on bogus TDY assignments to different posts in different towns. He billeted in Amburg, Hamburg, Augsburg, Illesheim and Fuerth on the outskirts of Nuremberg. The local cadre quartered him in a room to himself while others in the building shied away from him.

George no longer trusted his contact, Kenneth Pedderson. He suspected his last two assignments were Pedderson's personal vendettas. Killing a man with a throwaway revolver and taking up-close photos of the body were above-and-beyond the call of duty as far as he was concerned.

There was no evident threat warranting the killings and Pedderson didn't even try to give him a reason. The first few killings, especially in Vietnam, George was sure were warranted assassinations because most of them were Vietnamese working both sides. The ones in Germany were supposedly communist spies. Then he thought, why not just capture them?

This last assignment, where he didn't actually kill anyone, really soured him. "If our man leaves the helicopter and can't get back in, make sure he never talks." Pedderson knew damn well this man, Real-Bad, wasn't guilty of anything. George was pissed that Pedderson considered a good American soldier expendable. He would have killed all of the communist soldiers rather than kill one of his own. The hell with the consequences.

Things worked out all right that time, but he wondered about the next time, and the one after that. He still had a year left to serve.

A week later, he called his XO, Major Barwell, who was his intermediary. George said, "Sir, I am done with killing for Pedderson. I am Regular Army."

There were several seconds of silence. "Are you sure you want to back out, Corporal? Your enlistment isn't up for another year."

"Yes sir!"

"I'll get back to you."

The next day George received a call from Pedderson. "You can't quit Rickson, you shithead. Your ass is mine!"

"Fuck you Pedderson, I'm done!"

"You'll be dead in a month."

"You'd better hope so." George hung up.

He never heard back from Pedderson or Barwell. Two days later a runner brought him a packet he had to sign for. It was new orders. They were sending him to the Kien Long district, Chuong Thien Province, Vietnam.

CHAPTER 9

GEORGE HUNG AROUND NEAR A TEMPORARY AIRFIELD FOR TWO DAYS, re-acclimating to Vietnam, including the abbreviations. ARVN stood for Army of the Republic of Viet Nam, VC was Viet Cong (communist sympathizers), NVA was North Vietnamese Army and its soldiers were sometimes referred to as Charlie. PSP was Portable Support Platform and LZ was a landing zone. A medical evacuation helicopter was called a Dustoff and the floor of a helicopter was the deck. Most of it he remembered, and the rest came back while he waited for his assignment. It turned out to be more killing than he could ever imagine.

He found himself as a Dustoff door gunner to aid in The Battle of Kien Long. The UH1B helicopters flew in and out of hot LZs, picking up wounded ARVNs. There were so many NVAs hiding in the brush and weeds surrounding the area that he repeatedly overheated the barrel of his M60 machine gun. He was forced to swap the barrel back and forth in the mount with another one while wearing an asbestos mitten. One of the medics usually helped him on the way in to the LZ, but he was on his own during liftoff. They were too busy trying to save the wounded.

The medics would jump out as soon as the skids touched the ground, sometimes before. They immediately started helping the walking-wounded, and the ones they were dragging, aboard. George would still be firing out over their heads intermittently, pausing occasionally to lend a hand pulling some of them aboard. The noise was so deafening trying to talk was a waste of effort. Hand signals had to suffice.

A couple of the medics would climb aboard with the first casualties, while the others would go back after the crawling-wounded. The din, accompanied by blowing dust, sticks and weeds gave everything a surreal atmosphere. Everyone at deck-level and below was covered with dirt, sweat and blood. Grips were so slickened by it the most secure hold was by clothing, although the Americans could usually wrap their fingers clear around the wrists or forearms of the smaller Vietnamese.

Inside, medics and crew, including George, would drag the bodies in from both sides toward the middle until they began to pile up. There was no time for stretchers. A crew member would signal a slash across the throat to stop loading. Sometimes, it seemed the Huey could barely lift off. Once airborne, the smells of blood, gut, urine and feces wafted through the hold and escaped to atmosphere. The various liquids drained off on both sides.

When they landed, the patients were littered into the beds of three-quarter-ton and deuce-and-a-half trucks. Sometimes an arm or a leg would be thrown in with them. Everyone was in a daze and not noticeably bothered by it. To George, the trucks were gut wagons.

* * *

On his third day of Dustoff, a medic was hit in the leg while assisting a wounded ARVN sergeant. They both went down only ten feet from the door, so George jumped out to help. He grabbed the left arm of the medic and hoisted it up over his head and onto his shoulder. The medic came up, still clinging to the ARVN with his other arm. When he did, a grenade hit the ground at the feet of the ARVN. George twisted away and dropped toward the ground, dragging the medic with him.

CHAPTER 10

GEORGE'S BODY WAS BLOWN THROUGH THE AIR IN A TANGLE WITH the body of the medic. He hit hard, lay there stunned, and then gathered his senses in a daze. Unable to move, he looked around, deafened, not yet sure what happened. Images seemed to pulse at him and then recede. Then he realized his Medivac was lifting off without him. Up, away——and gone. His vision seemed to flash on and off and there were blanks in his memory. He looked at the torn and gutted body of the medic beside him and found that he, himself was covered with gore. Then the pain hit, like someone had sunk an axe into his torso. It doubled him over and he rolled onto his left side in agony and drew up his knees in a fetal position.

He would have screamed, but the pain was so intense he couldn't draw a breath. Only short bursts of air squeezed through. Then he did scream as a second blow from the invisible axe hit him. When the scream died out, he could recall the grenade hitting the ground. His mind couldn't grasp what happened immediately afterward though. It never entered his head to wonder what happened to the ARVN sergeant. Between waves of pain, he realized other NVAs would be coming to finish him off and he wouldn't be able to do anything about it. He didn't even have a weapon. Then he remembered the .45 in the flap holster on his right hip and reached for it. His hand came away bloody. The pistol was gone.

Play dead ran through his mind. He knew it wouldn't be long before death was a reality. With the helicopter gone, silence came rushing in as if a vacuum had sucked away all sound. Normal country sounds of birds, mammals and wind noises were absent. Only the ringing in his ears from the blast remained.

George supposed a roaring in his ears was what death would sound like... unless he screamed his way to Hell. Then he heard a rustling in the bushes behind him and knew that Charlie was coming for him.

Maybe I can grab one of the little bastards, maybe even his rifle. Or, if there's more than one, take him with me...break his spindly little neck as I go.

He lay as still as death itself, ignoring the pain even though it sent ripples up and down his skin from chest to knee. His hearing was now acute, despite the ringing in his ears. Now he knew what Pedderson meant when he said, "You'll be dead in a month." The bastard. George lost consciousness.

A continuous, thumping, thunder sound awoke him. He was disoriented as the noise overpowered the ringing in his ears. He opened and closed his eyes, trying to get them to focus between bursts of agonizing pain, mostly in his right side, so he was surprised to distinguish a man looming over him. Beyond the blurry vision of the man was a hazy vision of a helicopter. He thought he was hallucinating, but the man shouted. He was a big man, with a handlebar mustache and a Texas accent.

"We thought you was dead. Your uniform is the only reason I came over here." He reached down and yanked at something down around George's feet.

A wave of pain stabbed George in the leg, and he hollered out, "Bastards!"

The medic grabbed George's right arm and half-lifted, half-carried him to the Dustoff. The pain was still so intense he couldn't straighten up and only hopped on his left leg. George did notice three stripes on the sleeve and the man's nametag. It read Vogt. A minute later, they were airborne. Another medic looked down at George, a big black one, a corporal. His nametag read, Harrison. "You gonna make it boy," he said with a big grin, as he held up a syringe. The voices came to him as if his head was inside a drum. The medic plunged the needle into George's right thigh, and the lights went out.

George woke up in a field hospital. A tall, thin American nurse with black, shoulder-length hair and a stern look stood beside him. "Where am I?" he asked.

"Brinks BOQ, Saigon. Do you know what happened to you?"

"Yes, I was blown up by a grenade. I thought I was done for."

"Well you're not. Do you know what your injuries are?"

"No, I jut remember pain and more pain."

"Well, a piece of shrapnel went through your side. Another hit your right thigh, but you're going to pull through."

"I was covered with blood and guts. I don't remember anything about my leg."

She reached out and squeezed his hand. He squeezed back, "Well most of it wasn't yours. You were the lucky one." Then she pulled away and left.

He looked around and found he was in a large room filled with over twenty cots, all occupied. He gazed at the others and saw a couple of them looking at him too. A few seemed out of it completely. A couple just lay there moaning. One man was talking incoherently to an invisible person. It was obvious from the outlines under the sheets that some of them were not all there. Parts of them were missing. The ones looking at him had the thousand-yard-stare and didn't speak. He wondered if he had it too.

Then another figure loomed over him. One he had seen before. It was the medic, Vogt.

"How you feeling, Gunner?"

"Numb and dumb, man. Thanks. What the hell happened?"

"I thought you knew. The ARVN was blown to pieces. We lost one of ours too."

"Thanks again, I thought Charlie was coming for me."

"He was, and our gunner took him out. You were reaching for your .45 when I got there."

"It was gone."

"No it wasn't. The shrapnel nearly severed your pistol belt and the whole works was down around your knees. The tip of the holster was sheared off by the piece that hit your thigh, but the pistol's OK. I had to drag the belt down over your legs. I'll hold onto them for you.

"I talked to your crew, Rickson. That ARVN sergeant dropped the grenade deliberately. He was VC and knew he was dying. The sucker and wanted to take y'all with him."

Vogt continued while George tried to think back over the events. "My name is Steve. Write me when you get on your feet again." He handed George a slip of paper.

"My name is George. Thanks for saving my ass, Steve."

He got another Texas smile. "Part of the job. So long, George."

Not long after Buck Sergeant Vogt left, another man stepped up to his bed. This one was wearing fatigue pants and an olive drab tee shirt. Despite the lack of insignia, George instinctively knew this man was a doctor. "I'm Captain Downing. How are you feeling Corporal?"

"Not too bad, considering, Sir." George said. "What's the verdict?"

"Liver damage and a piece of shrapnel in your thigh. The good news is there is a Naval vessel nearby and they have a first-rate surgeon on board. I could remove the shrapnel in your leg easy enough, but the liver is another matter. A big piece of metal passed clear through you and without opening you up, I can't tell how extensive it is. So… I'm sending you over to the Navy in the morning. They'll take good care of you."

"What do you think will happen after that, Sir?

"Well, Corporal, you have a million-dollar wound with the liver damage. You will get a Purple Heart and you'll muster out."

"Thank you, Sir."

"Don't thank me, thank God." He left without waiting for a reply.

* * *

George went through his surgery while the ship was underway. The surgeon told him afterward he had lost fifteen percent of his liver. "The good news is that it will grow back. The liver is the only human organ that regenerates. It will take quite some time, and you will have bouts of intense pain during the regeneration. We are going to start weaning you off the morphine anyway. Get used to the pain, Soldier. It means you are still alive."

* * *

They transferred George to another ship in the Philippines, and transported him on to Hawaii. From there, Military Air Transport Services flew him to an Army facility in Seattle. He spent a month in the hospital there. It seemed to him that most of the time was spent waiting for his medical records to transition from Army to Navy and back to Army again. While he was there, he recuperated enough to walk with a cane. A night nurse named Donna helped too.

Donna looked quite a bit like the nurse in the field hospital in Vietnam, tall and slender with black, shoulder-length hair, but this one didn't have a stern expression. She had a lopsided smile that only needed a little coaxing. A straight, diagonal scar, about an inch long, on her cheek made her smile uneven. But when she did smile, the scar looked more like a dimple.

When he met her, George had left his room with the help of a walker and staggered fifty feet down the hall. He stopped to rest and her arms reached around from behind and grabbed onto the walker. His ears were still ringing from the explosion over a month earlier, and he hadn't heard her coming.

"I'm your nurse for the night, Soldier. I won't let you fall."

He looked around at her in surprise. "Well I might want to with you around."

She laughed, "Let's keep going."

He wasn't sure if she meant walking, or with the repartee, but he straightened up and resumed his walk. "Thank you, Nurse. It's nice to know you've got my back." He had mixed emotions about the open-backed gown he was wearing. At least he was wearing his white Army boxers.

"Which room are you in?"

"Two-fourteen."

"Let's go to the end of the hall and then I'll get you back into your room."

He couldn't help but look back over his shoulder at her with a grin. He made it to the end of the hall and back, but his forehead and upper lip had broken out in a sweat by the time she helped him back into his bed.

"Where are you hurting?"

"My side, my back and my leg. That's all."

She smiled again. "I'll come back later with some lotion."

It was midnight before she made it back. The other two men in the room were snoring and the one TV was blasting away. George wasn't paying any attention to it. He was contemplating what he might do for a living after his discharge.

The nurse arrived and checked his pulse and blood pressure. Then she had him lay on his back while she listened to his heart with a stethoscope. After that, she told him to roll onto his left side while she listened to his heart from the back. Before placing it on his bare back, she blew gently on it to warm it.

"My name is Donna. Do you go by George?"

"Yes, I'm pleased to meet you, Donna. I'm so used to being called by my last name, or Corporal, I almost forgot what my first name is."

She rolled up the stethoscope and dropped it into a pocket on her dress. Then she patted him on the arm and said, "Roll on over on your stomach and I'll put some lotion on the wound on your back." As she worked, she said, "I think we can take those stitches out tomorrow."

"Good, when I'm not hurting, I'm itching."

"That's a good sign. Now hold still while I put a towel on the mattress." A few moments later she said, "Now roll over onto you back." While he was rolling back, she held onto his gown so it didn't drape onto his oiled back, then she flipped it on over across his front. She left him like laying partially exposed while she pulled a straight chair over beside the bed and lathered the wound on his thigh with lotion.

She began massaging it in with her thumbs and the heel of her hand. When she used her thumbs, both hands were on his thigh, almost too close for comfort. Laying there exposed from the chest down, except for the boxers, he forced himself to think of other things.

Even though there was pain with the massage, it felt good too. All he could think of was the girls in Germany, their soft warm bodies and their hairy legs. "Stop, Donna!"

She didn't have to ask why, she knew. She gave him a little pat on the knee and capped her jar. "OK George, It looks like you're feeling better."

He yanked the gown back over himself. "Yes, thanks. I have to go to the bathroom now."

"Do you need any help?"

George's face was red. "No, I can handle it." He realized what he'd just said and his face turned even redder. He saw a smirk on her face as she turned to leave. By the time she reached the door, they both burst out laughing.

"What! What! What!" came from one of the other beds. Two beds over, a man sat up and looked all around. Then he lay back down. George looked back toward the door. Donna was gone. George saw her twice more that night, attending to other patients. She only gave him a fleeting smile as she passed by.

The following morning, a bald-headed doctor in his fifties and a grim-faced nurse, wearing first lieutenant bars, inspected his wounds. The doctor said, "Very good," and left. The nurse stayed and removed the stitches without speaking. George could only guess at the numbers. He thought twelve in the back, twenty in the front and maybe another sixteen in the thigh.

That night, George waited until later before starting his walk down the hall. He made better progress than he had the night before and reached the end of the hall unassisted. He turned around, only to find Nurse Donna in front of him.

"Don't quit now, George. Go on down the side hall on the right. Go all the way to the double doors. I'll be right behind you." When he reached the doors and turned around, she stepped aside for him to pass. As he went by her, still gripping his walker, she brushed her fingertips lightly along his arm from wrist to elbow. "Doing good, George."

Both halls were long and he was straining to keep going without stopping before reaching the comfort of his bed. She stayed right with him all the way and only gave him a pat on the knee as he covered up. "I'll be back."

The massage that night was almost the same. She was more gentle on his unstitched wounds and lingered longer. George didn't speak. When she finished, she said, "We'll go farther tomorrow night." George only smiled at the double entendre. She gave him a pat on the knee and the little lopsided smile on her face lingered on her way out. The other patients slept on.

CHAPTER 11

GEORGE KNEW SOMETHING WAS GOING TO HAPPEN WITH NURSE Donna that night. He hoped he could keep himself under control. It was six weeks since he spent the night in a German hotel in a giant sleeping bag. A college student, petite Helena from Malta, was an energetic, boisterous lover: gorgeous but hairy. She was another he would never forget. Still, it was May and abstinence for more than a month was a long time.

This time George went down the hall, turned the corner, and moved along all the way to the double doors. A sign he hadn't noticed before caught his eye. STOP! Authorized Personnel Only. He hadn't seen the nurse, but when he started his turn, she was there.

"Don't turn, go on through the doors." She stepped ahead of him and held one of them open. "You look stronger tonight, George. Ready for more exercise?"

"I am." She directed him on down along the hall past the first few doors, and into one on the right. The room contained a single, full-sized hospital bed, rollaway bed-table, two chairs, a small table and a walk-in closet. "What is this," he asked?

"It's for senior officers and visiting dignitaries. We don't have any senior officers and tonight you are going to be the visiting dignitary."

He lay on the edge of the big bed while she sat in a chair beside it, massaging his thigh. Flat on his back, he let his hand hang down over the side and moved it around until he found her leg. He began stroking it in sync with her massage. She edged closer, facing him, so her knees were up against the mattress.

He heard her breath quicken and looked over at her. Nurse Donna's face was flushed, her eyes were closed and her lips were parted. He moved his hand higher. He had never encountered a nurse without panties before: at least none he was aware of.

George could barely walk by the time he started back to his own room. But the next day he was much better and started walking with a cane. He received two more special treatments in the visitor's room and then the Army transferred him back across the country.

He knew he would miss Donna, but accepted the change. He wondered if she would miss him too.

A few weeks later, and a year early, they released him from active duty on a medical disability. The doctor there ordered him to check back into a military hospital for weekly visits. Later, it would be monthly visits just to check his progress.

* * *

Not sure what he wanted to do; George took a train ride to Chicago. The old station in Indiana had been shut down and his railroad superintendent father transferred to the Randolph Street Station in the Loop. His father, Pete Rickson, met him at the station and drove him out to Skokie, where his parents had bought a house. George told his father right up front he was just there for a visit and wouldn't be staying long. Pete just grunted, but his mother was very happy to see him.

In his accumulated mail was a letter from William Real-Bad and one from Steve Vogt. Vogt's letter had an APO return address, but Real-Bad's showed a Portsmouth, Virginia address. He opened Vogt's letter first. Sgt Vogt had been wounded, shot in the leg, only thirty days after George saw him last. He was en-route to the same hospital where George met Nurse Donna. George wondered if Steve would have her as his nurse and if he would be one of her visiting dignitaries.

William Real-Bad was in Virginia, helping a friend. George decided to go to Virginia.

CHAPTER 12

Will

ABOUT HALF IN THE BAG, I STOOD ON A CORNER JUST OFF BROADWAY in Manhattan in the middle of the night. I was contemplating either going on back to the Murray Hill Hotel or more drinking to enhance my celebration of severance from the US Army. It was early April 1964 and they let me out just two days shy of a full three years of service.

After several hours of uneventful barhopping, it was a toss-up. Then I heard a sound approaching that nearly always turned me into a different animal——the tap-tap-tap of high heels.

When I was working or studying, I turned off the drinking and tuned out the women, although I was never totally unaware of them. Now there was nothing on my plate or in my immediate future and I was tuned in, but wondering if it wasn't a lady-of-the night. I had nothing against them, but the concept just didn't ring my bell. And, after spending time in other countries, where prostitution was rampant, I was wary of venereal diseases.

Not many people were on the street after 1:00 AM, so I was certainly curious. I leaned against a corner lamppost, which gave me a good field of view, but there was no one in sight.

She marched out of an alley halfway down the block, which I took as a bad sign, but turned in my direction. Her steps never faltered when she spotted me and she kept to the center of the wide sidewalk.

My initial impression was shapely. When she came closer, I could see she was a redhead, wearing a pink, knit dress. The mass of hair floated in a pile on top of her head, with a single, large ringlet escaping down past her left ear. It jiggled as she walked toward me, as did nearly everything else. She had handles everywhere without being overly abundant.

A shiny black shoulder bag hung alongside her right hip and she discreetly shifted it just enough that I couldn't see her right hand. I already knew she was streetwise the way she kept her distance from the buildings and what few parked cars were there.

It was a nice, warm balmy night for New York and when she came close enough, I said so with a smile.

She stopped a few feet away and asked, "Are you the night guard?"

This gal was street smart. She had me off balance with her comment and knew it. My own instant appraisal told me she wasn't a hooker. I laughed and she walked on past me, veering only slightly to keep her distance.

"I was just out here contemplating my future and enjoying the nighttime," I said without moving from my lamp post, "It got better when you came by."

She stopped and turned halfway back around and I saw an even better profile view of her in the knee-length dress and black spike heels.

"Well, if you had stopped at one more bar you probably would have seen me at work. Now I'm on my way home and I'm not going to stay out here long."

We stood there appraising each other for a few moments, then both of us laughed.

"Is that a short-term or long-term future you're working on," she asked?

"Mostly long-term," I answered.

"Come on and walk with me a ways Night Soldier. You can protect me from evil." I stepped forward and she reached out and took my right arm. I doubted I'd be protecting her from evil though.

We walked and talked, and then descended into a subway station. Under the fluorescent lights, I could see her eyes were a strange, jade green and that she was older than me, maybe as much as ten years older. The difference didn't matter.

When her train arrived, she said, "Well, are you coming on or going back?" I didn't have a choice. I stepped into the train with her.

* * *

She lived in a tiny, third floor, three-room apartment in Queens. The old red-brick building held a white-goods supply store on the ground floor. I looked around before we ascended, and it seemed like a quiet neighborhood.

As soon as we were inside, she took off her heels one at a time by bending her knee and grabbing the spike. "Keep it quiet. The downstairs neighbors are sleeping," she said with her soft lilt as she turned to face me.

I was staring right into the top of those genuine red curls before lowering my gaze to those big green eyes. She had a plump lower lip and I wanted to kiss her right away, but I knew enough to wait.

"My name is Star O'Neal, and don't you forget it. Now what's your name?"

"William," I responded. "And you can call me anything but Willy or Billy."

She took my hand and led me through the little kitchenette to a short sofa, barely bigger than a love seat, in the equally small living room. She gave me a gentle push onto the sofa and turned away. "I'll make us some coffee."

I said nothing and she didn't seem to expect an answer as she set her shoes on a chair and disappeared into a bathroom just off the kitchen. I wanted to keep a clear head with this gal, so I was glad of the coffee.

The coffee was good and we chatted casually at her small table while we drank it. She seemed perfectly capable of sizing me up while doing most of the talking, and that suited me. I noticed one of her upper front teeth was slightly crooked while she was telling me her fifteen-year-old daughter lived with her. The tooth gave her an impish little-girl look as her lips moved. I was also thinking oh-oh when she told me about the daughter, but then she told me the kid was visiting her father and wouldn't be back for four days.

Coffee finished, I used her bathroom while she took care of the cups and saucers. Inside, her stockings hung on one end of a rope spanning the length of a big, claw-foot cast-iron tub. The sheer nylons were thigh-highs with seams, which perked me up even more. I washed my face with cold water before leaving.

When I came out, she was sitting on the sofa watching me with one thumbnail tickling the bottom of the crooked tooth. I sat beside her and quick-as-a-wink she hopped back up, spun around, and hiked the dress up to her hips. I couldn't have torn my eyes away from her if I wanted to. She poked her knee up between my legs and straddled my left leg. At the same time, she grabbed my neck with both hands for support.

"Now, one wrong move and you've had it, Buster."

I figured the right move was to grab her waist, and it was.

She was a true redhead with the pale skin and light freckles of the best of them. The quick glimpse I'd gotten of the white panties turned me into a jelly-filled puppet.

Star wasn't the prettiest woman, but she had plenty of sex appeal. Her features were just a little on the coarse side, her skin somewhat porous, and her face just a little lopsided. She was a few pounds over-weight too, but she was mine for the moment and I wouldn't have changed a thing about her.

An hour later, and nearly passed out, I realized I heard voices, grunting, and thumping. Star was sitting upright on top of me in the full-sized bed, moaning and talking gibberish with her fingernails digging into my pectorals. I was holding onto her arms just above the elbow to help her keep her balance. The thumping and one of the voices was coming from underneath me.

We finally realized what was happening. The old man in the apartment below was banging on the ceiling with a cane or broom handle. Something woke him up.

I stayed for three nights. Star went out every morning and returned with a newspaper and fresh bagels or muffins. Practicing my previous occupation, I nosed around, starting with her other purses and inside her shoes, where women are prone to hide things, while she was gone. I had already looked into the black, patent leather purse while she was bathing. It had a vertical zippered pocket that opened on the end, and inside, where her hand disappeared, was a husky switchblade knife with a four-inch blade.

Her little apartment contained scattered fragments of her whole existence and I found nothing with my snooping that indicated she was anything but what she said she was. I didn't touch areas obviously belonging to the daughter. When Star returned from her outing, she was always in jeans, flats, and a shorty-nightgown top under a light jacket.

* * *

I was in Star's bathroom getting ready to hit the street when I heard a crash behind me. I yanked the bathroom door open only to find my exit blocked by the kicked-in entrance door. I saw enough through the gap though. An incredibly tall man held Star by the hair while she clawed frantically at her purse.

I kicked the door back the way it came from, hard enough to break it and bang it into the man's leg, but he didn't go down.

I broke free just as he hollered, "I told you!" and punched her in the face.

As tall as he was, he probably only outweighed me by about ten or fifteen pounds, but it didn't matter. He must have thought I was the daughter. His back was to me and I grabbed him by the seat of the pants and the blossomed-out back of his shirt and heaved upward. He helped me by instinctively leaping in the same direction to escape the pressure on his crack. I slammed his head hard against the nine-foot-high lath-and-plaster ceiling and he caught it at an angle trying to look back down at me.

Before he could collapse, I spun him toward the door to shove him through it and he collided with another man I hadn't even seen, knocking him down. I shoved my man on out and down the stairs just as the other one was coming up off the floor with a knife.

I was ready for him too, but it didn't matter. His focus was on me and he lunged upright into Star's switchblade. It caught him right below the Adam's apple with a solid thunk, stopping him dead. The impact tore the knife from her hand.

I grabbed him by the hair and the belt as he was falling, and heaved him tumbling end-over-end down the stairs to land on top of his friend.

She started for the bathroom, but I stopped her. "Leave the blood, we're calling the cops." Her nose was surely broken and the lower half of her face covered in blood, but the bleeding had almost stopped. "They're probably both dead, so tell me who the big guy was?"

"An old boyfriend," she gasped, and then collapsed into my arms shaking like a leaf.

I dragged her to where I could reach the phone and called the cops myself using the number on the emergency sticker. Afterward, I put her on the sofa and said, "Just tell the truth, except that your old boyfriend brought the switchblade and dropped it. If you say that we'll be all right." Quickly, before the police arrived, I went down to the landing to make sure the tall one's neck was broken. Just as I finished, a door on the second-floor landing opened a crack and an old man's face peered out at me. "Just checking for a pulse," I said.

His wizened old face flashed a smile that vanished even quicker. "Uh huh, I never did like that mean sum-bitch anyway." He slammed the door shut.

Later, I heard him tell the cops they heard the ruckus but didn't open their door. "Scared to," he said.

We were OK after our grilling by the cops, but they kept me longer. They poked around at hanging the switchblade on me, but I told them I thought the tall one dropped it. Her story matched so they gave up on the questioning.

Later in the day, they came back with a couple more cops to show them the shallow dent and the long crack in the hard, lath-and-plaster ceiling. They even took pictures of it with a small flash camera. Two of them laughed and the other two just kept looking from me to the ceiling. When they left, the last man out clapped me on the elbow and said, "I've known him for twenty years and he was a real piece of shit. Thanks." Then he told me to hang around until after the inquest.

After they left, Star told me how she was glad he was dead. He slapped her and her daughter around whenever he came by, and took money from them both whenever he felt like it. He was the neighborhood bully and had been beating and taking from people his whole life. "You should have seen his face when you yanked him up in the air. He'd never been manhandled like that before. He was astonished."

As I finally left, I thought about how close I had come to not being there at all. Now two men were dead and her looks would never be the same, but she was probably more liberated than she had been in a long, long time. I hadn't initially meant to kill him, but when beating women comes into play it's a different ballgame. The manner in which Star told me goodbye told me our relationship was over too. I didn't blame her. She needed to find herself again.

* * *

Since I was under orders from NYPD to stick around for a few days, I camped out at the Murray Hill Hotel. With nothing else to do,

I went to the USO and picked up free tickets from them for Radio City Music Hall and The Statue of Liberty. I visited the statue first. While on my way by ferry, I looked out over the water and saw debris floating over most of the surface. Most prominent were used condoms, more than I cared to count. A faint smell of sewage rose along with the typical smell of diesel oil and fish from a major waterway. I was disappointed that our greatest of cities allowed this to happen.

Lady Liberty herself was smaller than her base and when I climbed up inside, I found myself standing at the level of her throat while peering out through small windows in her crown.

Moving on, I rode the subways to the different Burroughs and walked the streets. In Midtown Manhattan, I passed an Arthur Murray's dance studio, and thought why not. I had gotten in some dancing in the past, but not much. While I was in France, a German girl named Inge taught me a simple dance step for fast dancing. She just called it Slop, but it worked for just about anything.

Girls and women of all ages love to dance and I loved women. I figured there would be plenty of them in a dance studio and I wasn't wrong.

A pretty woman named Stacey, who looked to be about thirty, with boy-short, gray hair and glasses took my money and signed me up. Despite the gray hair, which did look good on her, and the glasses, she was very classy looking, petite and shapely. Later, I found out she was married to one of the male dance instructors. The music came from records played by a dedicated disk jockey.

An interview was required, primarily on what I expected to learn and why. The price was high but I wasn't disappointed in the selection of dance partners. The women outnumbered the men four to one, requiring us to change partners frequently. They were working on box waltz and cha-cha when I entered so that's what my ninety minutes for the day bought me. It was enough.

One of the first instructions was; the man leads, always. The concept suited me just fine even though I knew I would need guidance from my more-experienced partners.

I was the youngest man there too, the rest of them ranging in age from thirty-five to sixty-five. I was not as well dressed either, wearing my chinos, lace-up, plain-toe oxfords and a sports shirt, with the tail out. At least the shoes were soled with leather, which worked well for dancing. Most of the men wore custom dancing shoes with higher arches and heels. I resolved to upgrade my wardrobe for social events.

All of the women were attractive and ladylike, even the heavier ones and the older ones. They were all dressed nice too, and all but one very tall woman were wearing heels.

It didn't take long to find out some of them were posers and some of them were not above cheating to get at the male partners of choice. With me being the exception, the men's age didn't seem to be a factor. Dancing ability counted most. Two of the women were after me right away and I caught vibes from a couple others.

Of the two women whose favor I'd garnered, one looked barely eighteen and the other was a blonde around forty. The young one was a real beauty with a flawless olive complexion, flashing black eyes and long glossy hair that hung in waves to her shoulders, continuing in ringlets for another six inches. Bright red lipstick accented the dark hair and eyes. She wore a reddish-gold sheath dress extending to her calves, but with a slit up one side to mid-thigh. She told me her name was Cecilia and I didn't even try to guess at her ancestry.

The petite, five-foot-two Cecilia always seemed to catch me when we switched to cha-cha, and she seemed to hold me tighter than the dance called for. The feel of her warm body, smooth skin and the exotic scent she was wearing had an instant affect on me. It was more of a faint, nutmeg smell, rather than a cologne smell. Until then, I hadn't realized how much of an effect scents have in sexual attraction. I was getting aroused just dancing with her and I had to will my mind away from it. She knew though, and her smile said she was pleased with it.

The five-foot-five blonde was an attractive, well-put-together woman wearing a white blouse with a frilly front and a flared black skirt that ended just below the knees. Her dance of choice was the waltz. She asked my name and told me hers was Esther. The waltz was my favorite of the two dances and I never would have considered it an erotic dance, but in a way, it was. Her scent was a light gardenia. It wasn't as enticing, but was still pleasant and appealing.

Esther and I became as one, every motion synchronous, our eyes locked, expressions neutral, only the lightest of touches guiding the next move. Despite the formality of it, I felt her feeling-up my triceps and lats. The fingers of my right hand cupped her back, and I could feel her well-filled brassiere through the blouse. Her body felt as firm as a teenager's. During the progressive moves, our thighs briefly slid against each other, enhancing the moment.

Near the end of the last waltz, she whispered, "Butterfly please."

When she reached the apex of her outward swing, her right leg rose gracefully, first with the knee bent and then with the foot extended, until her foot was higher than my head, her arm and fingers extended straight out toward her toes in what I thought of as a ballet move. Now I understood the purpose of the flare on the lower part of the skirt.

I was on the wrong side of her to get a good look, but I knew she was showing me what she could do. I intended to find out more about her abilities later.

During a break in the dancing, we adjourned to a seating area with tables. Sitting to my right, a handsome, dark-haired man in his thirties introduced himself as Vince. I shook with him but wasn't sure where this was going since Cecilia was sitting on his other side. I hoped I wasn't treading on his territory. He looked like Mafia, which didn't make things any better.

I noticed the surprise in his eyes when he felt the calluses on the edge of my hand, but he didn't say anything about it. His was callused too, but not as much. Instead, he complimented me on my progress and asked if I had ever been to the Tuxedo Ballroom on Eighty-Sixth Street. I assured him that I hadn't and he asked if I would like to go the following night with him, Cecelia and another woman.

The woman to my left nudged me and said, "That would be me. I'm Mickey."

Mickey was a dish too, a few years older than Cecelia, and I quickly accepted the offer. I wasn't sure who would be with whom and I had noticed a wedding ring on Vince's left hand. Neither of the girls was wearing one. They laughed at my expression and Vince said they would pick me up at my hotel at 8:00 o'clock. The ladies filled me in on what to wear, and I was glad to hear a tuxedo wouldn't be required.

I stood on the sidewalk at the red zone in front of the hotel lobby the following night. Promptly at 8:00, a new, black Cadillac pulled smoothly to the curb in front of me. As soon as it stopped, the rear passenger door opened slightly and I took the cue and pulled it on open. Cecelia waited for me to join her inside. Mickey sat in the center up front, next to Vince.

I asked if any of them were related. I needed to know if she was Vince's sister, niece or whatever. Mickey laughed from the front. "No, we are all just good friends."

I didn't ask any more questions. Cecelia reached over, grabbed my hand, and slid over next to me. She said, "Vince is taking us all out to eat. I hope you like Italian."

"Love it," I said.

From the front, Vince, in his smooth, mid-town voice said, "Do you drive, Will?"

The question caught me by surprise. "Drive what?"

"Car, automobile?"

"Oh, sure. I was afraid you meant golf or something. I drive cars, trucks and boats. You name it. I drive it. I was driving a tow truck when I was sixteen."

He turned halfway around in the seat to look at me with a surprised look on his face. "No shit!"

The girls looked astonished too.

He was veering over the line and Mickey must have poked him because he turned to the front again. "You want to drive my car?"

"It's a beauty, but no thank you. I don't know the streets or the traffic patterns here. I'd hate to ruin the evening by wrecking your car. Besides, my stateside license has expired."

"No worry about that," He was silent for a few seconds and then he said, "If you decide to stay in New York, I could find work for you."

I didn't think he was talking about driving. "I'll keep that in mind."

He fished around in a pocket while he drove and then handed me a business card. I tucked it away without reading it. It might come in handy some time. Later, I saw it only had the name Vince and a telephone number on it.

I had a great time that night, dancing and cuddling in the back seat with the lovely Cecelia. After the dance, he drove us into the country for miles before stopping and parking in a secluded area out near West Point. Later, I drove us back into the city with Cecilia up front while he cuddled and smooched in the back seat with Mickey.

They dropped me off at the hotel after 2:00 am and I never saw the beautiful Cecilia again. I still didn't know what the relationships were. They lived in a different world from me.

* * *

The next afternoon I had a date with Esther for some personal dance lessons. She picked me up in the same spot, but in a gold-colored Mercedes. We left New York and crossed over into Connecticut on a very scenic drive. While she drove, she told me her husband was a sixty-five-year-old workaholic and he was away on a business trip to Canada with his twenty-eight-year-old secretary. She left me to fill in the blanks on my own.

She said, "Did you enjoy your date last night?"

That one caught me by surprise. "How did you know about the date?"

"I've seen them do it before. I'll bet they took you right back to your hotel afterward."

I didn't mention the little side trip. It didn't matter anyway. Then she said, "Cecelia is only sixteen. Mickey is nineteen, and Vincenzo is thirty-six, and married."

I had no answer for that, so I didn't say anything. I was just glad things hadn't gotten out of hand. She didn't say any more about it and I was glad about that too.

We made one stop at a little country store where she bought a few groceries. Apparently, we were going to a house or apartment.

The tour ended at a chalet on a wooded bluff overlooking Long Island Sound. As we wound up toward it through the trees, I noticed the glass front jutted out from the bluff and had an open, roofed balcony. As an escape route, one would have to drop into the tops of fir trees twenty feet below. Not impossible, but nothing I would want to try either. The view was awesome and no other houses were visible.

She left the door we entered through wide open, went straight through to the glass front and opened the sliding door there too. A nice breeze quickly extinguished the slight musty smell.

We entered into a hall and passed a bedroom with a private bathroom on either side. The front half was completely open and contained a kitchen, sitting area and an oval glass dinette set to one side of the glass door. There was barely room to dance, but we wouldn't be doing much dancing anyway.

Esther fixed us omelets, sausage and toast for an evening meal. She made mine with four eggs. There was a glint in her sky-blue eyes when she handed it to me.

While we ate, she told me she wanted to be an acrobat when she was a little girl. In her early teens, she wanted to be a ballerina. When she entered college, she studied economics, became an accountant, and eventually a CPA. Working as a CPA was where she'd met her husband. Neither wanted children and now they co-existed, but lived separate lives.

We sat out on the balcony and talked for a while after we ate and then she said she needed to work out. I raised my eyebrows and she continued, "Would you like to watch?

"Yes, I would like very much to watch."

She drug mats out from a closet and spread them on the floor just inside the windows and across the doorway from the dinette set.

Afterward, she went into a bedroom and closed the door. A few minutes later she returned wearing a sleeveless gymnast's leotard and ballerina slippers. On the balcony, she performed contortions while staying on her hands and feet. It was an exotic performance. Her body was firm and toned without being too muscular and her breasts were almost too big for the top.

She could pull either leg up alongside her head while standing on the other foot. Some of her movements were flowing and similar to tai chi, then she would take a stance with other movements similar to Yoga. She stood in front of me facing away and brought her head and arms down and between her knees, her bottom near my face and her upside-down face gazing at my crotch.

From there she flowed back upright, turned to face me, and did the same thing backward. I couldn't believe she was so supple.

She had been moving in and out through the sliding door, but now the sun was going down and the air was chilling. We retreated to the inside and closed the doors. Afterward she switched on mood lighting and began posturing on the mats. I sat in a chair right in front of her and watched. She stopped, laid on her back and pulled her ankles behind her head.

"Would you like to have sex like this?"

I was on her in a heartbeat. As I suspected, there wasn't a hair on her body.

I burned up all four eggs that night, and four more the next morning. We both knew there probably wouldn't be a repeat performance. She asked me if I was going to stay in New York, but I pleaded that I had to return to Florida to settle an estate.

I thought about returning to the dance studio, but I never did.

CHAPTER 13

BACK IN NEW YORK, I FACED A TWO-DAY WAIT FOR RADIO CITY MUSIC Hall, so I wandered the streets talking to vendors and seeing the sights. I bought a newspaper the morning of the show and sat down to read it on a bench in Central Park. Almost immediately, an article caught my eye.

A prominent New York citizen, Abel Winneke, was berating the court system for releasing the felon who kidnapped his thirteen-year-old granddaughter. The kidnapper was indicted after a short inquiry, despite not disclosing the whereabouts of the granddaughter.

During the incident, Winneke's daughter stepped out of a cab in front of the kidnapper's vehicle just as he grabbed the kid off the sidewalk. The cab drove off while the mother ran up and clawed at the man's face trying to get him to release her child. He punched the mother and knocked her down, yet managed to drag the girl into his van even though she fought back too. Another man drove while it disappeared into traffic.

The mother and a lady friend with her were both able to quickly identify the kidnapper at the local precinct. The friend had written down the van's license plate number before belatedly trying to help. A trace on the number listed it as stolen... from a Pontiac.

The abductor still had the scratches on his face when he was captured twenty-four hours later. Police were reportedly still searching, but neither the van nor the other man was found.

Wilbur Peebles, the kidnapper, secured his release under forged court documents supplied by a phony lawyer.

What caught my eye was the photograph accompanying the article. Standing on the courthouse steps next to Winneke was a man I knew, Phillip Henrik, a US Army Two-Star General. I had saved General Henrik from a major embarrassment and possible loss of command. I caught his wife sleeping with a communist sympathizer. It was out of line, but I accosted the General directly with photos. He sent his wife back to the States and I didn't report the incident.

Henrik was in civilian clothes, but I recognized him anyway. The General wasn't likely to forget me and I knew how to reach him. It was time to go to work, time for business. I called, but couldn't reach him until the next morning.

Thoughts of the kidnapping were on my mind but I enjoyed the show regardless. Rockettes danced on the raised wings on each side to music from an unseen source. I felt privileged sitting close, and just below one of those wings. Esther kicked as high as any of them, but her body was more muscular.

As the Rockettes danced their way back beyond the wings, the entire orchestra providing the music slowly rose from a pit in front of the main seating area. It was quite a show.

What was most surprising was that after a wonderful performance by the dancers and the orchestra, they all disappeared and were
replaced by a giant movie screen. From there until the end, we watched
a first-run movie. It seemed anti-climatic after the live performances
and thoughts of the kidnapping I couldn't shake.

CHAPTER 14

THE KIDNAPPED GIRL'S GRANDFATHER TURNED OUT TO BE GENERAL Henrik's brother-in-law. Henrik set up a clandestine meeting between me and Abel Winneke.

We met for lunch in a small, Jewish Deli in Queens. "What can you do the police can't," he asked.

"You mean after I find Peebles, don't you?"

"If you find him, but yes."

"I won't turn him in. He will tell me who his partner is and where your granddaughter is. I can't guarantee her safe return though."

He just stared at me for a few seconds before saying, "Her name is Penny."

I nodded, "I'm not hampered by the same constraints as the police. I hate psychopaths and pedophiles."

He seemed satisfied with what I said and we struck a deal—no money up front. Then he said, "You will need expense money."

He started to write a check, but I said, "No, just cash. It will be safer for both of us. I'll call you tomorrow." I didn't mention an amount.

We met again the next day at the same place, but earlier. He handed me a sealed envelope and I pocketed it without looking inside. Later, when I did open it, I found $2,000 in fifties and twenties, far more than enough to get started. I rubbed two of the fifties together with my thumb and forefinger and thought about those first two fifties, the ones I took from Hiram Walker's watch pocket.

After lunch, I bought a newspaper, and rode the subway up to the Bronx where I purchased a used car, nothing fancy, nothing hot-rod. A 60 Studebaker Lark 2-door sedan caught my eye. With a six-cylinder engine and column shift with overdrive, it was all I needed. The tan color made it even more nondescript. It turned out to be a better car than I had ever driven before and I decided to keep it for a long time.

Finding Peebles turned out to be easier than I thought. The police had already caught him once, so they were no longer looking for him with the same enthusiasm. The General obtained a list of his known associates from a contact in the NYPD, along with the areas where he hung out. Even without knowing, New Yorkers could tell where a man was raised by his speech. Each borough and each area of Manhattan formed a unique dialect. I could pinpoint most of them myself from men I met while in the Army.

Several people heard Peebles speak when he grabbed the girl. Most people detest child molesters anyway, and I only had to ask around at a few bars to find his newest haunts. It was just as well I owned a car, because he had one too. His was a 54 mercury 2-door hardtop, red with a black roof, easy to spot and easy to follow.

When I did spot it, he was driving and I hoped he would lead me to a house or building where the kid was. Instead, he drove out to New Rochelle and then on past. Eventually, he drove toward the coast and into an area of deserted warehouses. I knew I had been spotted and hoped I wasn't running into an ambush.

I zoomed up behind him, forcing him to act. He turned out to be more stupid than I thought. He was a big, tough, city man and he thought he could handle it himself, so he stopped.

Peebles ran back to my car with a lug wrench half raised in his right hand. I rolled down my window before he reached it, more in hopes that he wouldn't break it, and put my scared-face on. Instead of trying to hit me, he put his left hand above the door and stuck his face in the window. "OK Asshole, wha-chu following me for?"

I grabbed his shirt at the throat with my right hand and jerked his face forward, banging his forehead against the doorframe. He pushed away with his left hand and I shoved too, adding to his momentum. He staggered backward clear across the other lane, tripped over the curb, and went down hard. He must have banged his head, because he was still stunned when I reached him. His lug wrench was six feet away. One good punch to the chin was all it took to knock him out.

I drove away with him locked in the trunk, hands tied behind his back with his bootlaces, and his belt doubled around his ankles, strapped tight. I stuffed one of his dirty socks in his mouth and tied it in place with the other one. The whole process took less than two minutes.

His Mercury was still running and I drove past it without stopping, certain someone would find a use for it. I had to drive a ways to find a secluded enough spot and he started to thrash around back there. I slammed on the brakes and accelerated a couple times to soften him up, and then the rear-seat backrest popped open and he rolled out behind me.

"Listen, Stupid!" I shouted over my shoulder as he started to rear up. "If you don't stay down and lay still, I'll put an eye out with your own pig-sticker." He lay still, but I could hear muffled sounds as if he was trying to talk. "Can it! Roll back into the trunk," I hollered. He shut up and rolled back.

I had found the hunting knife in one of his lumberjack boots, neither of which I expected to find on a city boy. The knife was the only weapon I found other than the lug wrench. I figured they would both come in handy, and they did.

A wooded park appeared ahead of me and just as I was ready to slow down and turn in, I noticed a police car coming toward me. I drove sedately on and they passed with barely a glance. It was close to dusk and I would have to find somewhere else soon.

With just barely enough light left, I turned into what looked like an abandoned farm. The driveway was overgrown, but not tall enough that my car would leave a trail. I drove on around behind the small, dilapidated barn and found the big door open. After I backed the Studebaker inside and shut it off, I stepped out and listened for any sound of man or animals... nothing.

I had to work by flashlight, one I put in the glove compartment when I bought the car, along with a pair of snug-fitting doeskin gloves. Peebles was a big man with a shock of course black hair. Cleaned up, he might have been considered good looking, but not now. He had already pissed his pants by the time I rolled him out onto the dirt-and-straw covered concrete. It wasn't long before he shit them too. I didn't have to get too creative with the knife before he was ready to tell me what I wanted to know. He knew by then I meant business.

His partner's name was Everet Tollo and they had a prospective buyer for the kid, or one who fit her description. Tollo was the only one who had seen the buyer, "Some rich guy on Long Island named Windom."

After spilling all of that and giving me an address in Queens, I told him, "I'm going to leave you here now. You won't bleed to death, but if I find out you've lied to me, I'll come back and poke your eyes out with this knife." By then, he believed every word I said.

I couldn't risk going back though, so I rolled him over onto his belly and caved in the sweet spot at the base of his skull with the lug wrench. The blow caused his body to straighten and quiver. I was certain it killed him, but I gave him another whack just to be sure. There was no doubt then. He had $250.00 in his wallet, a driver's license and some small change. I kept the money. Two of the bills were fifties.

* * *

At 4:00 o'clock the next morning, wearing dark clothes, black tennis shoes and the doeskin gloves, I slipped the back-door latch open on the house in Queens and eased my way in. I parallel-parked two blocks away and scouted around the house. The only place I was able see anything in the house was through a venetian blind with a cracked slat near the bottom. All I could make out was a man dozing on a sofa, bathed in the light from an unseen television.

The back door of the older-style, single-story house opened into a large kitchen and faced straight down a hall. I could see the sofa pushed back against a doorframe on the left side at the far end. The man was reclined, facing forward to my right, with his chin on his chest. I passed a bathroom and a pantry opposite the kitchen, and a bedroom on the right. The door was open and I noticed an unmade bed, a dresser, and a wooden wardrobe.

Within ten feet of the sofa, I stepped on a squeaky spot on the floor. The man sat upright and swiveled his head in my direction with a confused look on his face. "Who the fuck are you?"

I quickened my step.

He fumbled on the sofa beside him and came up with a revolver—far too late.

With only tree-quarters of a turn to target, the point of the lug wrench hit him right between the eyes. It sounded like someone dropped a melon on the sidewalk. Both he and the revolver fell back onto the sofa. I wanted to grill him, but he was dead when I reached him, the lug wrench at least three inches deep into his head. As for looks, this one could have been a twin to Peebles, but he was a strawberry-blonde with the skin coloring of a redhead. I reached over the sofa and pushed the door open a few inches. I could see the girl curled up on a cot. She was under a blanket on her side, facing away from me.

I could see she was trembling and I said, in as soft a voice as I could muster, "You will be all right now Penny. Stay right where you are. The police will come for you in a little bit, and then you'll go home." I hated leaving her there, but she hadn't seen my face and I wanted to keep it that way. I eased the door shut and turned back to the dead man.

A driver's license, $276.00 in cash and a phone number filled Tollo's wallet. The number matched the one I'd gotten from Peebles. I took all of his money too and replaced it with a hand-printed piece of paper containing the number and the name—Windom, Long Island $3,000.

To confuse the medical examiners even more, I turned the lug wrench a full turn so the bottom of the hole would be flat, not wedge shaped. It was easy enough to turn, but hard to pull out. I was forced to step on his face. The black-blooded hole made it look as if someone had driven a half-inch bolt into his head. I avoided it with my shoe.

As I left, I said to the bedroom door, "Stay right in that room Penny. They will come and get you in a just a couple minutes." I went to a pay phone three blocks past my car and called the police. Afterward I called Abel Winneke and told him to stay home, the police would have his granddaughter in a few minutes. I returned to my parking space, facing away from the house. In only a couple of minutes, a police car went screaming by. I sat up and drove away.

I didn't hear from Winneke again. A day-and-a-half later, I called General Henrik. In the interim, I thought about what all had happened. If someone else had been in the house with the girl and the man, it might have had a different outcome. In the future, I would need someone to back me up, someone good, and not squeamish. I thought about Robert Cee and then the shooter, George Rickson.

The night before, trying to fall asleep, I thought about myself too. What had I become? I had killed four men and tortured one of them, yet I felt no remorse for doing so. Was I bound to wind up in Hell? I didn't know. Was I wrong in doing what I did? Again, I didn't know. I believed that my actions prevented others from becoming victims of those evil men. I just hoped I wasn't becoming evil myself.

* * *

Henrik answered the phone himself. He said, "I was hoping you would call me and not Abel. They tapped his phone because they thought the kidnappers would call him. They are suspicious of the anonymous call too." He paused, but before I could say anything, he continued.

"Abel's granddaughter will be fine, and they are overjoyed. They need an address to send you a package. Thank you, Will. We won't forget you."

I gave him the number of a Post Office Box I rented earlier. Nothing showed up in the newspapers for two days. When it did, not only was the girl back home, but police and FBI agents raided the Long Island home of banking executive Raphael Windom. The FBI arrested Windom and rescued another child from his child-pornography filled mansion. It turned out Windom owned the house in Queens as well.

The day following the newspaper article, I received two packages with bogus return addresses. There were no names mentioned, but one was from Winneke, with $20,000 in cash and another from General Henrik with $5,000. The one with $20,000 had only a brief note. "I wish it was more but couldn't raise it without suspicion."

I had been in New York for a month, hoping to hook up with Robert Cee but he was at Fordham in Manhattan, going for a law degree. Too many things happened during that month and it was time to leave. I decided to return to Florida to see what was left of my family.

CHAPTER 15

WHEN I WENT BACK TO FLORIDA, I WAS STILL HAVING OCCASIONAL back pains so I found a chiropractor and had him check my back. The X-rays showed a cracked vertebrae at L4, mostly healed, and a misalignment between L3 and L4. I probably caused the misalignment by hoisting Star's old boyfriend to the ceiling.

The chiropractor advised me to tough it out and move carefully for two more weeks. Afterward, he would be able to put things back in place and take pressure off the disk and nerves.

I didn't have much to go back to Florida for. My little sister was married to an OK guy, and pregnant. They would never have a whole lot, but he was a steady worker and would always have a job. He was currently a plumbers' apprentice. My uncle, a bachelor, had died, and my only cousin had moved away. Asking around, I found out my friend Larry was killed in a car wreck while drinking. Eva, the lover I would never forget, was unreachable and most likely unobtainable. I mentally wished her well.

I decided to visit a girlfriend from even farther back in time, Trudi. She was a hot little number I'd been playing hide-the-weenie with back when I was a senior in high school. After asking around, I heard she was as hot-to-trot as ever, but married now.

I stopped looking but then bumped into her by accident a couple days later. She wanted to pick up the game where we left off, but I wasn't interested. I gave having a fiancé as an excuse, but Trudi's looks had gone to seed too. Besides, I didn't want to get involved with a married woman anyway.

Still in Florida and at loose ends, I visited a few bars in Ocala. I talked with a few guys I knew from school, all of them married and already getting fat. As I was leaving a biker bar called The Hog Pen, someone took a shot at me. It missed my head by a few inches and peppered the back of my neck with stucco dust. I felt the sting of it before I heard the shot and was already dropping when the shooter fired again. The second shot hit where I was a moment before, and I crawled back inside the bar.

A couple of biker fools ran out the front door to see who was shooting, while others ran out the back, no doubt to see if their Harleys and Triumphs were OK. I stood up and went to the bar, where I grabbed a handful of bar napkins. I slapped them against the back of my neck where the stinging was escalating and told the bartender to call the cops. At first he refused, "We don't want cops in here."

"Listen asshole, the shooting was outside and I'll wait outside. You want me to tell them it was inside?"

He called them.

Two cops took me to the emergency room and ushered me right in, a speed record in my book. After scrubbing cement dust and tiny stones out of my hide with a small, brass brush, the Doctor doused some fiery antiseptic on the area so I wouldn't forget it was there. Then he slapped a bandage over the mess and taped it down with enough tape to pull out my short-hairs when it came off.

They kept me at the police station for another two hours grilling me about who would want to shoot me. I didn't have a clue, and told them so. "It had to be random."

"Bullshit," said the sergeant. I only shrugged. I was in there long enough to find out I had been shot at with a .22, probably a rifle. They found where the shooter fired from, a roof across the street and down a few doors. The building was empty and they never found any empty brass.

"Don't leave town," the sergeant said. "On second thought, leave town and don't come back." They left me to find my own way back to my car, probably hoping someone would take another potshot at me so they could gather more clues.

I didn't have to walk far. A fairly new, gray Chevy sedan pulled to the curb beside me and the window powered down. I was ready to hit the ground if a barrel poked out the window, but I was still less than half a block from the police station, so I held off. From inside the car, a familiar voice said, "Need a ride?"

It was my old acquaintance, US Marshal Jerry Smith. He was the only one in the car, so I opened the door and slid in beside him. "Were you shooting at me?"

He shut off the car and laughed, and then so did I. He said, "No, I wouldn't have missed," and we laughed again.

"I heard you were back, William and I have been trying to catch up with you. A couple different people have been asking around about you. It can only be about the still-missing Hiram Walker. We haven't found him, wherever he's planted.

"I heard one of the askers is a shirttail relation to Walker, but I haven't found which branch of the family tree, or why he would be interested. "You want to tell me?"

"Like I told the sergeant back there, I don't have a clue."

"When did you get out?"

"A little over a month ago."

"Where have you been since then?"

"Well, I was discharged in New York and I have a friend up there, so I stuck around for a visit."

"What does you friend do for a living?"

"He's a student at Fordham, going for a law degree." That seemed to surprise him and he was silent for a minute. He said, "I heard about a kidnapping and a recovery up that way. The two kidnappers were killed in strange ways. You know anything about that?"

I laughed, "No."

"OK William, what I know is this. When you are in the vicinity of bad people, they die or disappear."

"New York is one hell of a big city. All sorts of strange things happen up there."

"Yes, I guess that's so. Take care William, I don't want to go looking for your killers."

With that, he started the car and drove me right back to mine. He deliberately glanced at the New York plate and grinned as I stepped out.

I drove back to my hotel room to pack my bags. After things cooled down, I would come back and try to find out who had it in for me. Then I stopped to think things over.

Whoever shot at me was an amateur. Marshal Jerry Smith was right. At close range, a professional wouldn't have missed. I thought back over my two return trips to Florida. My liaison with Eva was too long ago and too distant. That left Trudi.

She told me her married name when I bumped into her, and it didn't take long to track her down. They lived in a trailer park a couple miles out of town. I didn't know her husband, or even what he looked like. When I found the place, a rusty dodge pickup sat in the dirt driveway next to an old tan Desoto, the one she was driving earlier. Someone had brush-painted Slut in crooked letters eight inches high on the back of the trunk lid with black paint.

The back window of the truck cab displayed a rifle rack, complete with rifle.

I parked several spaces away in a vacant lot and walked back. The side windows were open on the truck, so I walked up on the side opposite the house trailer, reached in, and grabbed the rifle. The Stevens Model 87 was still loaded, with one in the chamber.

Just in case he had another gun handy, I stayed on the far side of the truck and set the rifle down in the bed. Then I moved back to the front and pounded down on the hood several times with my fist.

He came bounding out, barefoot and shirtless and leaped off the one-only porch. "What the fuck!" His hands were empty so I stepped out from behind the truck. He jerked to a stop and said, "It's you."

Now I knew for sure he was the shooter. I closed the distance to six feet within two strides. "What the hell were you shooting at me for? Do you want to spend the rest of your life in prison?" In my peripheral vision, I noticed Trudi standing in the doorway watching.

He saw me glance her way and turned his head back to look, then snapped it back my way. I was already three feet closer. He was younger and about an inch taller than me, but lighter, with a mop of light brown hair and a see-through mustache. He held his ground. "You screwed my wife!"

"Like hell! I wouldn't touch her greasy ass with a ten-foot pole."

He balled up his fists so I slapped him hard alongside the face and knocked him down.

"Don't even think about getting up until I'm gone." By then I only felt sorry for him. I saw tears well up in his eyes, so I gave him a moment. "This can be over or you can wind up dead or in prison. Either of them won't be worth it."

He nodded his head, so I continued, "tell me it's over and it will be over. Otherwise, go to hell."

He stayed there on his back, but propped himself up on his elbows. "It's over."

Certain he was done, I returned to the truck, grabbed the rifle and emptied the tube onto the ground. I ejected the chambered round, and carried the rifle back to my car.

He stayed in place, so I laid the rifle on the ground behind my back wheel. Both wheels on my side crunched over it as I left. At the least, it had a broken stock. It might have a bent barrel too.

* * *

When I returned to the motel and stopped at the desk to check out, the clerk handed me a message slip. I, Robert Cee, and a couple others used phone messenger services. I thought it was from Robert.

CHAPTER 16

THE MESSAGE WAS FROM A MARINE FRIEND, WARREN HOWELL, I MET him during a special weapons seminar in the Philippines. Warren's Marine buddies tagged him with War Howl. The message stated he needed help and included a phone number. The kind of help wasn't specified.

When I called, I was surprised to find the number was for the Portsmouth Naval Hospital across the Elizabeth River from Norfolk. While waiting to get through to him, I wondered what happened. I knew it wouldn't be good.

When he answered, I said, "Hello War, what the hell are you doing there?"

"Hell is right, Bad. I lost both legs at the knee. I'll be here for a long, damned time."

"What happened?"

"Nam, machine gun took me down. Half of our landing party was killed outright. Piss poor intel. That was three months ago, in

March. It was pure luck I fell into a hole. Otherwise, I would have had my brains blown out too, like Simpson beside me."

"Oh man, I'm sorry it happened. I never went over there myself, but I lost friends who did. How can I help you?"

"It's my grandparents. They need help and my parents aren't up to it. Granddad owns, owned, two TV shops, one in Portsmouth and one in Norfolk. Now both of them are shut down. He didn't care much for the way Norfolk had grown with highway overpasses and heavy traffic, so he hung around his shop in Portsmouth and let a manager take care of the bigger shop in Norfolk. That one carried high-end brands like RCA, Curtis Mathes, David Bogen and Marantz. It was geared primarily to sales, the smaller one in Portsmouth catered to service. It was still a big operation. Both shops employed ten to twelve people."

"Each one?"

"Yes.

"The manager in Norfolk bled the place dry and was filing false claims for service. He falsified purchase orders for merchandise he never bought and kept the money. When it was all about to fall down around his ears, he issued worthless paychecks to the employees too." Warren stopped to catch his breath.

"What happened after that?"

"Granddad called the manager, Cletus Arnold, over to his shop in Portsmouth and confronted him. Arnold hit Granddad with a radio and beat him almost to death. When Grandma tried to stop him, he hit her with Granddad's cane and broke her collarbone. He took all the money from the cash drawer and forced her to open the safe. Grandma had expensive jewelry in there too, along with cash, checks and bonds."

"How much did he get away with?"

"Probably fifty thousand in cash from Norfolk, and twenty from Portsmouth. I have no idea on the stocks and bonds."

"Fifty grand sounds like a lot of cash for a TV shop."

"Granddad pounded the streets for years, selling personal products to colored folks in Portsmouth and Norfolk. He studied correspondence courses on basic electronics and TV repair through National Radio Institute at night. They scrimped and saved. All they have left for income now are a few small rental houses."

"Personal products?"

"Yes, Pomade, hair straightener, skin lightener, wigs - stuff like that. They all knew him and he could go anywhere."

"What happened to Arnold?"

"He lived in an apartment in Norfolk. The police had him cornered, but he jumped out of a second story window onto a shed roof and escaped on a stolen bicycle. He knocked down a twelve-year-old kid to get it. They don't know where he's at now."

"Hang in there, War. I'll be up to see you day after tomorrow. I'll do what I can."

After I found a hotel room in Norfolk, I called Warren's grandfather in Portsmouth and explained that I was trying to help as a friend of Warren's. He gave me Cletus Arnold's address in Norfolk and described him and some of his habits. Howell said Arnold was thirty-five years old and single. He was tall, with wavy brown hair and a prominent nose. He was gregarious, hung out in bars after hours, always with a woman, although he seldom kept the same one for very long. The last one Howell knew about was a Mexican woman named Nina. She worked in a Norfolk real estate office, but Howell didn't know which one.

While I had him on the line, I asked about the rental houses, saying I needed a base to work from. He perked up at the possibility of a rental.

"Well I have two places available, one is a duplex in Craddock, empty on both sides, and the other is an upstairs apartment in Portsmouth. It's in poor shape."

"Is either side of the duplex furnished?"

"One side of the duplex is, yes. They skipped out on the rent two months ago and left everything. It's a mess."

The duplex appealed to me for a variety of reasons so I arranged to meet him there the next morning.

Mr. Howell stood medium height and was slightly overweight with thinning, gray hair slicked back on his head. He wore a threadbare brown suit with an un-ironed shirt, giving him a rumpled appearance. White socks showing over the tops of his dusty black oxfords completed his ensemble. His wooden cane was the right kind. Once I knew him better, I would show him how to use it as a weapon, one that could be deadly.

While we talked, he alternated between picking his teeth with a wooden toothpick and sucking air through them with a squeak. Still, he was so friendly and relaxed I couldn't help but like him. He pulled his toothpick from his mouth and spoke. "You look pretty young for this."

I stretched the truth a little. "I'm a combat veteran and I've been all over the globe."

He studied me for a few seconds before saying, "I see it in your eyes." That ended the conversation.

I went through both sides of the duplex while he stayed outside and let me look. Afterward, I told him I would like to rent both sides.

He seemed surprised, so I said, "I will have some friends coming to stay with me off and on. I'll put them up on the other side. Mostly, they come down to fish. I have cash and I'd rather keep it off the books." He liked the cash idea and we struck a deal. He would keep the utilities in his name for both sides. Somehow, I would have to find a way to cover my expenses. I hoped Cletus Arnold was still around. If he wasn't, Norfolk and Portsmouth would have to provide ways to make money.

I moved into the furnished A-side the next day. I also hired Howell's seventeen-year-old granddaughter Judy, War's cousin, to clean the place up and come by once a week to do laundry and cleaning. Judy was a short, chubby little gal with brown eyes and straight, black, neck-length hair with bangs. I could tell she had some American Indian blood in her too.

Despite the weight, she was as cute as a button and seemed to know it. She kept trying to stand too close to me and I finally told her I was seeing someone. It didn't deter her a whole lot, but she finally caught on nothing was going to happen between us.

Over the next few weeks, I replaced the furniture a piece or two at a time, and moved the originals to the empty B-side. That side I kept private, added blackout curtains, and changed the locks.

* * *

During the next week, I toured the area surrounding Arnold's address in Norfolk, an area of mid-scale rental houses interspersed with project apartments. A manager of a thriving business should have been able to do better. There were several bars in the neighborhood and I started working my way outward from the closest one. With only a name and description to go on, I didn't hold out much hope of finding Mr. Cletus Arnold. I started with bartenders and barflies, then anyone in his age range who looked friendly. Most of the people I talked to were friendly enough, but didn't know him. A few just glowered at me and a couple told me to get lost, in not so friendly terms. I ignored them and went on.

It was a borderline area, both White and Hispanic, so I asked around about Nina. No one professed to know her and most of them just shrugged as if they didn't understand. The surrounding areas in Norfolk were still pretty much segregated between Black and White and I saw public drinking fountains labeled 'White' and 'Colored'. Even the YMCAs were segregated.

I got lucky in the sixth bar I visited. The bartender knew him as a semi-regular and a womanizer. "If he didn't have one, he was looking for one, usually Navy wives." The bartender moved away to take care of business for a while. I thought about what he'd said. I noticed more than one young woman looking me over in passing. I hadn't thought about the Navy, and how many young wives were left in port while their men were out to sea—a playground for any hungry wolf.

The bartender came back when I tipped my empty beer glass toward him. When he brought my draft refill, he said, "I heard him talking about gambling a few times too."

"With anyone in here now?"

"No, and we don't get into anything illegal here. Just saying."

I thanked him and he moved on. Halfway through my second beer, I headed back to the men's room. It was in an alcove to one side of the hallway in the back. Men and Women doors faced each other in the alcove with the women's out of sight of the bar area. When I opened the door to leave, a pretty, young Hispanic woman stood facing me with her back to the opposite door.

"I know something about Cletus Arnold. Don't speak now, just call me in one hour. She handed me a slip of paper and pushed her way backward through the door. I left without finishing my beer, a practice I learned along the way. Never give strangers an easy opportunity to dope your drink. An hour later, I called the number from a pay phone a mile away.

Someone picked up the phone, but no one answered. "You gave me this number," I said.

There was silence for a couple seconds before she said. "Who were you looking for?" I recognized her voice.

"Arnold. Are you Nina?"

"Yes. What do you want him for?"

I wanted to talk to her in person and I had a feeling she wasn't enamored of him, at least not anymore. "Nina, I want to talk to him about business. I will pay for information."

"Does he owe you money?"

"Not me, someone I know."

"How much will you pay?"

"Forty dollars if you help me find him. I won't tell on you."

"Fifty and I will help you."

"OK fifty, but tonight." She gave me a business name and an address closer to the river. "One hour," I replied.

Scotchy's was a combination restaurant and bar crowded with sailors in uniform and a number of women making choices. Overall, the women appeared five to ten years older than the sailors.

I stopped just inside the door looking for Nina, but didn't see her, so I moved on in and found a small table. Someone pushed me lightly on the shoulder from behind, and there she was. Previously, when I saw her in the bar, she was wearing jeans and a baggy blue top with her hair tied back. Now she wore a red, knee-length dress with a wide, black, patent-leather belt and black heels. The dress was not a hip-hugger but not full either. It buttoned up the front to her throat and accented her figure. Her wavy black hair glistened in a rainbow of colors from the neon sign on the other side of the window. She looked delicious.

"Did you ask me for a dinner date, Mystery Man?"

"Yes."

"Let's cross the street."

We crossed over to a restaurant named Roy's and were soon seated in a somewhat secluded booth toward the back. She wanted to sit facing the room, but so did I. I didn't know anyone in Norfolk, but I had been nosing around. We compromised and both sat on the same side, me on the outside. We weren't pressed tight together, but I could feel her thigh against mine.

"Are you expecting someone?" I asked.

"No, I've never been to either place before, but I've heard about Scotchy's"

"Oh, you like to look at the sailors?"

She laughed, "No, I didn't want all these old women looking you over in that other place."

I laughed. The waitress came and I ordered a Heineken. Nina ordered a red wine. From there we fell into small talk. I decided not to question her about Arnold until after the dinner. A dinner date with a dressed-up, pretty woman was something I hadn't done in quite a while. I was surprised and a little leery, falling into it so easily.

I was pleased she didn't seem to be a smoker and only smelled faintly of a nice perfume. I asked her straight-out if she smoked.

Faint lines appeared between her eyebrows before quickly disappearing in what I took to be a slight frown. She shook her head no. "I don't like the smell and I don't smell it on you. I didn't see you smoking in the bar."

I was surprised, because I hadn't seen her in the bar before she handed me the note. "Oh, I don't smoke and I don't know how I missed you in there, Nina. You are very pretty."

That awarded me a beautiful smile, and we moved on. She never answered and I surmised she was with someone. I let it pass——not my business.

She told me that she had suspicions about Cletus Arnold right from the start. He became obnoxious when she wouldn't let him into her apartment or go to his. "He is good looking but was too friendly, too flirty with all the girls. He became abusive when I told him I wouldn't go out with him anymore."

"Physically abusive?"

"No, but he called me some vile names."

"So, where is he now?"

"Oh, I don't know, but he had a new lady friend last week, a skinny, thin-lipped, narrow-nosed dishwater-blonde."

"Wow, that's a mouthful."

"Yes, she has big bazooms too."

That one made me bust out laughing.

Nina said, "Her name is Cynthia Leggit. I know where she lives too."

That caught my attention. "How do you know?"

"She rented her house through our agency."

Nina was the receptionist at the real estate agency, but also going to school for her license. I gladly paid her the fifty dollars. We made another dinner date as a personal date, just two people getting to know each other. I was happy about the whole afternoon.

CHAPTER 17

CYNTHIA LEGGIT LIVED IN A SMALL, ONE-STORY HOUSE JUST ACROSS the railroad from the river, no doubt one of many constructed for railroad workers during the forties and fifties. The house needed maintenance and the yard needed mowing. I doubted a man like Cletus Arnold would be up for hand tools or yard work. No one answered my knock at the front door, so I went around back. As soon as I stepped up onto the open back porch and my footsteps thumped across the boards, I heard a boom, thud, thud; a pause and then it was repeated—boom, thud, thud. I called out but no one answered.

I knocked and the noise became more intense. I rattled the knob, but the door was locked. I looked around for another way in and noticed a piece of sheet metal laying in the weeds beside the porch. It was about six inches long and four inches wide, with one end cut at an angle. It was just right to slip a standard door latch, and my guess was that someone had used it for just that purpose before. I did the same.

I looked around for something I could use as a weapon, but didn't see anything, so I wiped my finger prints off of the sheet metal and tossed it aside before I went on in. The first thing I saw was a dead man sitting at a kitchen table surrounded by flies and still-drying blood. The house was small, probably about 700 square feet, so it didn't take long to find the source of the thudding. A blonde woman matching the description Nina gave me lay tied, spread-eagled on a full-sized bed with a metal headboard and footboard. She was clothed in a shorty nightgown top, but naked from the waist down. It was obvious she had wet the bed. The smell was of stale urine. Her thrashing around had been rocking the bed causing the headboard to bang against the wall.

Before stepping into the room, I checked the other bedroom and found it empty, as was the bathroom: at least for the most part. When I entered the room she was in, I closed the door behind me.

Someone had stuffed a pair of panties into the woman's mouth and tied it in place with one leg of a pair of pantyhose. They tied her hands with the legs of another pair and her ankles with cloth belts. I did have a small pocketknife, so I quickly cut her loose. Tears were streaming down her face and she blubbered like a baby when I cut her bonds.

I started to go back for another look at the dead man, but she grabbed my hand and pulled herself upright on the bed. She sat there on the side of the bed and sobbed with her face against my belly and her arms wrapped around my hips. I just hugged her shoulders and stroked the back of her head while her tears wet my shirt.

It took a full five minutes for her to calm down and release me. She asked for a glass of water and I went into the kitchen and filled one for her. I didn't worry about fingerprints. I was going to call the cops.

After she drank half of it, she spoke. "It was horrible. They waited for a train to go by before they tortured him. His screams! His screams!"

She hadn't seen what they did to him and it was just as well. She got her breath back and said two men with Halloween masks surprised them in their bedroom just as they were drifting off to sleep. One held a pistol and the other a shotgun. One tied her while the other kept the shotgun pointed at Cletus. Then they took him away and tied him up too.

While each one raped her, the other stayed with Cletus. She never saw their faces but they had brown skin. "They were wearing rubber gloves too, but I saw a tattoo on one's wrist. He had powerful hands and thick wrists with course, black hair."

"What did the tattoo look like?"

She started to get up and walk toward the kitchen. "I can draw it."

"No, you don't want to go in there. Just tell me."

"It was the face of a smiling sun, with outward points around it, about the size of a nickel. Now, can I at least go to the bathroom."

"No, you can't go in there either."

"But I have to go—bad. Number two."

"OK, I'll find something."

"There are pots and pans under the sink. Bring one with a lid. Paper too."

I brought what she asked and said, "Don't clean yourself in front. The police will have the hospital examine you."

"But why?"

"What if one of them has a disease? You need to know."

The implication silenced her.

The killers had wired Cletus Arnold to a wooden kitchen chair with armrests using baling wire. His legs were bound to the table legs in the same manner. My guess was one of them sat on the table to immobilize it while the other worked on him.

It was easy to see why they waited for the noise of the train passing by. They had cut off both of his hands with a hacksaw while he was still alive. The saw lay in the pool of blood by his feet. For insurance, they sunk a butcher knife between his ribs from the back, post-mortem. It was still in place. His detached hands were in the toilet.

They ripped the phone wires loose, but I was able to hook them back up, a simple thing for someone who had worked in intelligence. While we were waiting for the police, she told me he had gotten heavily into debt through gambling and was hiding out with her. She said Buster-Somebody's men were looking for him. Finding them hadn't been hard at all. I didn't tell her how I found them.

The cops came up with many questions I didn't have answers for. I spent two hours in the back of a patrol car while they milled around in the house and took turns grilling me. I told them I tracked him down because I paid him cash for a television and never received it. I used the Duplex A-side address as my own.

I never mentioned Nina during my talk with Leggit so they never made the connection. I just told them I heard people talking about him in the bars, and I followed the woman home a couple days before. "Arnold wasn't there so I waited and came back later. The back door was unlocked and I heard the thumping so I went on in."

It was after 11:00 p.m. when they let me go but I called Mr. Howell anyway and told him what happened to Arnold without giving him the gory details. He agreed to tell the police I had been living at the duplex address for a month if they asked. It turned out they never did ask. I also told Mr. Howell that even though they couldn't get any money back from Arnold, I would try to find out who had it.

"I'm not going to ask how you plan to do that," he said.

I called Nina and told her Cletus Arnold was murdered, and that I found his body. She only asked if I was all right. We still had an upcoming date and I could tell her more in person.

CHAPTER 18

I REVAMPED MY SEARCH, THIS TIME FOR BUSTER, LAST NAME unknown. I had to tread carefully because professional hitters like the ones who visited Arnold had to be part of a much bigger operation. I was mystified as to why I drew nothing but blanks.

I was in a restaurant named Mateo's in downtown Norfolk when a little girl about six years old, with shiny black hair and big brown eyes, crawled under my table, hiding. As she was crawling under, I saw fear in her eyes. She was staring at a man's leg protruding from another table. The table was around a corner from me, so only his extended ankle and calf were visible.

The child was so obviously frightened I motioned her to crawl under my knees while I unfolded the large, linen napkin on my lap and draped it over them.

The man's leg was encased in expensive slacks, hose and a leather leisure-shoe I know must have cost at least a hundred dollars. The shoe size appeared to be about a 13, two sizes larger than my own.

I could feel the child trembling against my knee, and I steeled myself for the possibility of discovery. From the murmur of voices, there were at least three men at the table, speaking mostly Spanish or Portuguese. Finally, the leg withdrew and the men left without me getting a glimpse of them. I knew better than to lean forward for a good look.

Once they were gone, the woman appeared through a curtain behind me. Her face held the same frightened look and her hand clutched a steak knife in a white-knuckled fist. She was nearly as tall as me, with honey-blonde hair, golden skin and almost-black eyes. Her hair hung in waves past her shoulders, a truly beautiful woman. She softly uttered a name, "Marisol."

The child crawled from under my table and rose to hug the woman. The woman stared at me as if daring me to make a move or sound that would expose them. As they started to draw away, I spoke, "I hate evil men."

My words and tone stopped her, so I continued. "Sit here and wait until they are well away."

"I can't," she replied. "I am supposed to be working here."

"It's obviously too dangerous for you here. I can help and I want to," I replied. She gave me a long, silent appraisal.

They left with me and I heard their story as we drove away.

The woman and girl were Cuban. They were held captive on his yacht and jumped-ship, fifteen feet to the water, to escape his slavery. His name was Bustamonte. She pronounced it Boosta-monte. Her name was Murta.

Murta said, "Bustamonte is a rich Brazilian with many businesses and a private army. They kidnap women and children for him, both boys and girls. He sexually abuses them and after he finishes with them, he passes them to his men before putting them to work in his factories and mines. We were lucky to be put to work immediately on the yacht, but soon they would have had their way with us." Her words didn't need any clarification.

I took them to the duplex and put them in the B-side with instructions to stay put and keep the blinds closed.

Murta said, "I don't know how, but some day I will pay you back."

"Don't worry about it. If you want to work some of it off, you can clean my side of this duplex and do my laundry. I had a girl doing it, but I'll call her and tell her not to come."

"Yes, leave your dishes for me too."

Afterward, I called Mr. Howell and told him I had a couple in the other side of the duplex and the woman would be doing my housework. He promised to let Judy know she wouldn't be needed. He seemed to be relieved about the whole thing.

The next afternoon, I awoke from a nap to check on Murta and Marisol and found them both gone. When I returned to my side, I heard voices from the street.

Marisol was on the sidewalk facing two colored men. There were other children playing nearby and they rushed to Marisol. From behind me, Murta whispered, "I need a gun." She had entered my side of the duplex from the rear. I hadn't seen her a minute before.

"Wait," I said. The babble of the children had attracted a few mothers. One admonished the men to leave, or she would call the police.

They withdrew and I followed them.

We were four blocks away and on the edge of an all-colored neighborhood before they noticed me. They turned and separated and I stopped eight feet from them. They were both taller than me, and rawboned looking. One was a high yellow; he had a blue farmer's bandana tied on his head, knotted in the back, the point loose on top with wooly orange hair sticking out. He had high, shiny cheekbones and a slant to his eyes. The other one was black as coal and his wild bushy hair wouldn't be contained by anything less than a steel pot.

Bushy said, "What the fuck, man! You lookin to get hurt bad?" This one sported a puffy face and bloodshot eyes. I could make out ingrown whiskers from a lousy shave.

"Where's Buster?" I could tell by the surprised look on both faces that they didn't have a clue who Buster was. I was glad of that. I followed with, "Are you pedophiles?"

Bushy still didn't have a clue, but the redbone did. He stepped forward. "You sayin we mess with kiddies?"

"Do You?"

He took another step, so I held my hands shoulder high, palms out. "What were you doing with the little girl back there." I could tell by his face he wasn't going to answer me, and I was ready for whatever he wanted to throw my way.

A colored boy standing on the sidewalk said, "She had his sista's ball, but we's just playin.'"

Bushy scowled at him but the other one saw me cast my eyes that way and thought he had an opportunity. He tried to sucker-punch me. He threw a pretty good right hook but found himself facedown on the sidewalk with his arm twisted behind his back. I stepped over him during the move and stepped down on his neck with my left foot. The judo hold on his wrist was painful and he couldn't get at me.

Bushy leaped toward me with a wild swing and I caught him in mid-air with a right cross. He flopped over and hit the ground, out cold. Bandana managed to pull his arm free now that I was only holding it with one hand. I removed my foot from his neck to keep from having it pulled out from under me and he jumped up.

He spun to face me and his jaw dropped when he saw his partner laying there, out cold.

"Want to try again," I asked.

A small crowd of at least three races was watching. I could see the turmoil on his face. He didn't want to risk getting put down twice in front of them. Instead, he said, "What you done to Clive?"

I knew it was over so I said, "Sorry man, but I didn't want to fight you both at the same time."

His head jerked back in surprise. Someone rushed over to bushy Clive and started slapping his face. Bandana turned toward him too, so I turned and walked away.

Ten feet back, Murta stood there behind a wooden chair, gripping the top rail.

"What are you doing with the chair?" I asked.

She had a flustered look on her face. She was also seeing me with new eyes. "I thought you might need some help, but you didn't. You are some kind of fighting man, maybe a soldier. I didn't see it in you before."

I laughed and picked up the chair. As we started back I said, "I was a soldier, but not now."

"Those men were not from Bustamonte. He hates black people. He calls them monkeys."

Then it hit me. The Buster Cynthia Leggit was talking about was Bustamonte. Those were his men who tortured and killed Cletus Arnold. A man with that many enterprises would be involved in money lending too. The professional hitters with brown skin, the man with the strong wrists and the smiling sun tattoo. It all made sense now and it was time for me to bring someone else onboard. I called and left a message for George Rickson. I was pretty sure I could count on him. I also needed to find another place to fall back on if things got dicey. A newspaper ad led me to an apartment in Portsmouth, near the hospital.

CHAPTER 19

George

GEORGE DIDN'T KNOW WHAT WILL REAL-BAD WAS TANGLED UP IN, but he knew there would be some risk involved. And probably money too. He thought back to when they met in Germany and the man they picked up over the border in Czechoslovakia. Will hadn't said, but George suspected his job would have included interrogating the man, no matter how. For now, he didn't have anyplace else to go. The Government would send his disability checks wherever he told them to. He still didn't know where he would settle though.

Carrying all he owned in his Army duffel bag, he rode trains from Chicago to Richmond. From there he rode in a Greyhound bus to Portsmouth. Will was waiting at the station when he arrived, and shook his hand with a firm grip, not squeezing hard, not trying to prove anything.

"Hey George," he said as he grabbed George's duffel bag and slung it over his shoulder. Let's go get something to eat and I'll start filling you in. I have money to cover your expenses if you need it."

"I'm OK financially for now and I needed to go somewhere anyway. Just hold off on the money."

They drove to a diner and sat in a booth near the back. Will managed to get a seat facing the front. George wasn't crazy about sitting with his back to the room, but he didn't know anyone here so he shrugged it off. Besides, Will had his back.

Will surprised him, "George, what are you going to do with your life?"

"Well, I hadn't thought much about it. Get a job somewhere, I guess."

"Doing what?"

"Most likely as a mechanic. That's what I went to school in the Army for."

Between visits from the waitress, they continued talking.

"Mechanical work is not what you were doing when I met you? You were competent with a foreign rifle and in a position of some responsibility with it. You were skilled as a medic too."

George laughed, "We do what we're told. You know that. Besides, what were you doing there?"

Will grinned at him. "Pretty much the same as you, but from a different angle. Some of us do this, and some of us do that. It works out."

"What's going on here? I thought you lived in Florida?"

"Not anymore, and you didn't call me from Indiana." George didn't reply, so Will continued. "I need to figure out what I'm going to do for a living too, but I don't have to rush into it and I don't think you do either.

"I was asked for help by a Marine friend who lost his legs in Vietnam. The help is for his grandparents, not him. They lost their small businesses to a crooked manager. I was hoping to get some or all of their money back, but the man was already dead when I found him."

"So where does that leave you?" George asked.

"Through happenstance, I found out the money went to a rich, crooked businessman from Brazil who has a satellite headquarters here in Norfolk. He's also a murderer, kidnapper and child molester, with a small army at his disposal."

"That sounds like a dead end as far as your Marine friend is concerned."

"Not if I can get enough from the Brazilian to get his grandparents back on their feet."

"So you intend to take him on, and that's where I come in?"

"You are the first I called. We may need more, even with you, if you're in. Either way, I'll cover your expenses coming down here."

"Not to worry about expenses. I'll have them wherever I go. Let me digest what you've told me. Also, I think we both need to think about legitimate occupations if we are going to step over the line."

Will just nodded, and George thought about it while they ate. Afterward, he said, "Let me get a newspaper and check out the local job market for mechanics. Can you put me up for a few days? I'll need transportation too."

Will paid for the dinner and drove them through Portsmouth to a quieter part of town, not far from the Naval hospital, where he pulled up in front of a two-story house. George noticed the name of the street was Webster Avenue and the houses along there were only a few feet apart. "Come on in and have a look," Will said.

They stepped up two steps onto a full width porch with a roof and entered an outer front door that Will unlocked with a key. Inside, a stairway ascended on the left and another door stood straight ahead about twelve feet in. He unlocked it too, but with a different key.

Will proceeding, they entered a large living room with a door on the opposite side-left, and a hallway leading farther back on the right. A set of pocket doors stood open on the front side.

Will stopped. "Go ahead and look it over, I've seen it."

George noticed that the original front room, or parlor, with the pocket doors, had been converted to a bedroom. Inside was a full-sized bed with a mattress and springs, but no bedding. On the side opposite the entry hall was a closet containing nothing but a few wire coat hangers. The door was standing open and he left it that way.

The door opposite the front concealed a bathroom with a stand-alone sink and a cast-iron, clawfoot tub. The tub had a plastic curtain suspended around it and a showerhead hanging over it. Above the sink, a recessed, painted-metal medicine cabinet with a mirrored front stood empty.

He proceeded down the short hall and found a galley kitchen containing a small table with two mismatched chairs. The kitchen ran parallel to the front of the house and a door on the left side led out onto a small open porch with a roof.

Three steps down led to a small back yard with a set of clothesline posts with wire lines. It reminded him of a similar clothesline from his teen years, one where a man died.

A-sidewalk led back toward the front of the house and alongside the neighboring house. There were no doors on this side of the neighboring house, but a high bay window extended out to where it almost hung over the sidewalk. More toward the front, the house he was inspecting also had a bay window, but lower, and the sidewalk veered out around it.

George reentered through the back door and found Will sitting in one of the kitchen chairs. "Damn," George said. "July in Portsmouth is as hot and humid as Vietnam. What about the upstairs?"

Will laughed. "Someone else lives up there and they might object." George sat down and Will continued, "I've rented the ground floor with an option to buy the whole property."

"Obviously, you don't live here."

"No, I am renting both sides of a duplex on the other side of town and I have a tenant in one side. I live in the other."

"Damn, you work fast."

"Right now my occupation is landlord. Why don't you move in here, rent free, until you've made up your mind."

"I just want to know more about you, Will. I have a feeling but it's not enough."

"Fair enough. I'll tell you some, and you tell me some. There's no one here but us right now. What do you want to know?"

"Where did you get the money for this, the car and the duplex? The Army doesn't pay that well."

"While I was up in New York a month ago, a young girl was kidnapped. It turned out she was related to a friend of a friend. I managed to find her and get her back. Both my friend, and his friend, rewarded me."

George thought about that for a couple seconds. "What about the kidnapper?"

"They didn't make it?"

"They? How many?"

"Two. And yes, I did."

"Shoot them?"

"No, I used a lug wrench."

George laughed. "A lug wrench! I love it. Were they the first?"

"No."

"Shoot any of them?"

"Well, I shot one in the knee, but it didn't kill him."

"But he died anyway, right?"

"Yes." A pause ensued for thirty seconds or more while they searched each other's faces, and then Will continued. "What about you?"

"More than one. And even before the Army."

His confession seemed to surprise Will. "Shoot them all?"

"No, but I don't want to go deeper into it for now."

"OK George. Do you want to go get some food and bedding for this place?"

"OK, but if we go shopping for bedding together, they'll think we're queer."

They both laughed.

Will drove George through the tunnel into downtown Norfolk and dropped him off to shop while he went looking for a pay phone.

George felt strange shopping for bedding, dishes and flatware, something he'd never done before. He bought three paper shopping bags to carry it all. While he waited for Will to pick him up, he ruminated on his existence before entering the Army. He realized that within his three bags was more than what many of the residents in Papertown owned. Papertown was a collection of tarpaper-covered shacks adjacent to his former home. He hoped their standard of living had improved as well, then remembered they were all gone. Papertown was gone too.

After Will picked him up, they drove to a Giant grocery store. It was so massive George found it overwhelming. He found it hard to believe so many food items could be found in one store, or one store could be so huge under one roof.

"How about some eel, or squid, or maybe some chocolate-covered ants?" Will asked.

"I ate all kinds of crap in Vietnam. I'm sticking to American food."

Both of them carried George's purchases into the apartment. Will said, "I see you bought a couple of books. That's good because you don't have a television or a radio. Call me tomorrow. There's a phone booth about a block-and-a-half away, straight down Webster."

CHAPTER 20

GEORGE FELT STRANDED. HE NEVER LIVED IN A CITY COMPLETELY ON his own before. The Army had his back in Europe and everything was temporary. Of course this was temporary too, but it felt different. He pored over the newspaper he'd bought on his excursion with Will, looking for transportation. Among his purchases were Norfolk and Portsmouth city maps and a Virginia state map. Working with them, he found a used car lot not far away, so he walked the twelve blocks back into town.

Along the way, he passed three Negro men, ages spanning twenty or more years, standing on a corner. The Army abolished the term colored from its vocabulary and referred to those of African ancestry as Negroid, or Negroes. George stopped and asked them if there was a YMCA nearby. The youngest, a man in his late teens or early twenties, started giving him directions, waving his arms this way and that. The oldest man was in his forties and bald on top. He slapped the younger man's hand down.

"Fool, he's looking for the white YMCA." He began with new instructions and pointed in a different direction. "It's a long way to walk, man. There ain't no White anything in this part of town." The younger man just hung his head, while the third one laughed.

While they were talking, George noticed a drinking fountain on the sidewalk, up close to a building. A sign mounted above it, said COLORED ONLY.

After the man finished his set of directions, George said, "Thank you. I can't believe all the segregation I'm seeing here."

The thirties-something man finally spoke up, "Ain't nothing gonna change anytime soon."

"I was in the Army and we fought side-by-side."

"Me too, Brother. Where you fight at?"

"They moved me all around Vietnam as a sniper. I was wounded at Kien Long." He could see new respect in the eyes of all three when he mentioned sniper.

The thirties-something man replied, "My name's Alphonse. I was shot in the ass in Korea, didn't hunker down enough. Froze it off before that." He held his hand out in front of his face, elbow bent and fingers extended. George matched the gesture and they gripped hands, crossed thumbs and gripped with fingers. They pulled their hands back slightly and briefly gripped fingers. "Alphonse," the man said. "I'm always around here somewheres."

George nodded, locked eyes with the man, and spoke his own name. He left and resumed his walk. He wanted a YMCA for the lockers they provided. He didn't want to leave everything he owned in an apartment where someone else had a key. He felt it was better not to leave everything in one place anyway, considering what he was about to get involved in with William Real-Bad.

George wasn't sure of his financial future, so he was looking for a cheap car. A yellow 1954 Chevy with a green top caught his eye. A salesman in his forties told him, "Son, you need to make a better investment than this."

"What do you mean, investment? I'm just looking for a car."

"I can sell you the Chevy for $250 but in less than a year you'll be trying to unload it for half your money. A low-end buggy like that just doesn't hold the resale value. Young buyers like you are the future car buyers, and most of them want something slick and fast. In another year or two, when this war is over, we'll be flooded with young men with money to spend. Let me show you what they will want."

George didn't let on he was one of those young men. He reluctantly walked across the lot with the man. The car the salesman showed him was definitely a step or two up. He was looking at a black 1957 Ford, Fairlane 500, two-door hardtop.

The salesman patted it on the hood. "This is the one you want. It has a 312-V8 Thunderbird engine in it, and it's low mileage. Take a look under the hood."

George did. The motor was impressive. The rest of the car was too. He had to ask, "How much?"

"Nine hundred dollars," the salesman said. He could tell by the look on George's face he was skeptical. "This fine automobile has suffered some damage. The older gentleman who owned it hit a small deer down along the Intracoastal. It took out the left front fender, headlight, grill and radiator. They're all new."

George looked the car over closer and saw a slight difference in paint color on the fender and some slight evidence of other, superficial damage.

"Let's take a ride," the salesman offered.

They did with George at the wheel. He had never driven such a powerful, smooth riding car and squealed the tires a couple of times taking off. It was far different from the small cars he'd driven in Germany.

"Easy on the gas, Son. You'll get used to it but this baby can burn the tires right off of it. It'll run like a raped ape out on the highway."

George was sold, but he didn't want the man to know it.

When they returned to the lot, he walked away and started looking at other cars. A 1956 Chrysler caught his eye.

The salesman said, "The Chrysler is a real dreamboat, and it's fast, but it's still a boat. You'd have to pay more for it than the Ford, but in two or three years its value will be lower."

After some deliberation and haggling, George bought the Ford for eight hundred dollars. He gave the man two hundred dollars in cash as a deposit.

"I'll tell you what," the salesman said. "I know you walked in here. For another $100 deposit, I'll let you borrow the Chevy to take care of your business. You'll have to bring it back in two days."

George agreed and left in the Chevy. After driving the Ford, he was even happier with the deal he'd made. The steering was sloppy, the power was far less and the ride was rougher.

The next day he set up a bank account and made a sizeable deposit, but kept out more than enough to pay for the car. While he was at it, he rented a Post Office box. He also rented a safe-deposit box in the bank and registered at the "Y" so he could rent a locker. Now he felt more secure.

After taking care of business, he called Will. Will was silent for a few seconds after George told him about the car and George couldn't imagine why he would be upset about it. Then Will said, "Buy the

Chevy too. It's cheap enough. Just don't get it registered. I'll reimburse you. We can use a third car."

"OK, I'll just tell them it's a surprise for a friend." He didn't know what Will had going on, but figured there might be a woman involved. When he visited Will in the hospital in Germany they were both impressed with the same shapely nurse and they talked some about women when they were alone. Will impressed him with the word callipygian, meaning a well-shaped derriere.

George had a passion for women but wasn't about to fall in love. Will liked them too and arrived at the same conclusion. Domestic life didn't appeal to him either.

* * *

George picked up his Ford the following Monday morning, and surprised the salesman by paying cash for both cars. He left the Chevy there, and would walk back and pick it up in a day or two. His first goal was to get a Virginia driver's license and get plates for the Ford.

George took care of his licensing and registration business by early afternoon and headed south out of town. As he cruised down U.S. 17 along the Intracoastal Waterway with all four windows down, he felt a greater sense of freedom than he'd ever known. He'd gone straight from his parents' home in a depressed area of Northern Indiana into the Army and had never driven a car of his own before. He thought back to the old Desoto he'd bought, but never got running, and laughed to himself. It was as if he was now a different person in a different world. He cranked up the radio and in a minute Freddy Cannon's Palisades Park blasted from the speakers. The song matched his mood as he tooled along the highway.

He saw several turnoffs leading to the canal along the way and decided to stop and have a look at the next one. From his map, he knew the Great Dismal Swamp lay on the other side of the canal. It was reputed to be over a million acres in size.

The next turnoff came up sooner than he expected. The turnoff was overgrown with knee-high weeds but there was still plenty of room to turn around. He parked and walked toward the water, mindful of snakes. Even if he didn't see any, he knew they were there. Closer to the water, he found a wide, short pier laid with heavy, gray planks perpendicular to the line of travel.

When he reached its edge, he saw it wasn't a pier at all, but a dock. Its counterpart rested on pilings on the opposite bank, with a small barge secured to it.

George looked carefully, but there wasn't a sign anyone had been in the area recently. The only sounds were the buzzing of insects and chirping of birds. The egress on the opposite side was overgrown where it disappeared into the brush and weeds. There were no buildings in sight and the trail just vanished.

The barge was large enough for a car or even a farm truck and he speculated that whoever used the barge as a ferry had another way out. He looked around for a few minutes longer before leaving to explore the next one.

The next stop was even more of a surprise. Aging gray boards descended in a series of steps down the steep bank and ended at a large, Corps of Engineers barge. George looked and listened, but, again, there wasn't a trace of anyone around. He decided to go out onto the barge for a better look. Weeds and vines obscured the steps.

One step from the bottom, a huge, brownish-green snake lay dozing in the afternoon sun. It's head rested at the edge of the step and he guessed half of it may still be in the water. George eased back up the steps without disturbing it. Later on, he found two or three similar docks along the way without barges, even though they showed signs of occasional use.

He got back in the car and continued south. After a few more miles, he came upon a building on the left with a sign painted on its false, squared-point front: "Pap's Truck Stop." In front of the building, but to one side, a pair of gas pumps stood in the gravel drive. A third pump stood alone fifty yards beyond the pair in front of the building.

Twenty minutes past the truck stop, he passed the North Carolina state line. Deciding he'd gone far enough, he turned around and headed back north.

George pulled into the Pap's Truck Stop parking lot, but parked far enough past the building so he wouldn't block the pumps. He noticed on his way in that the isolated pump was diesel.

The building had a raised floor with three wooden, open-board steps ascending to a small excuse for a porch. A wooden-framed, flyspecked, screen door opened outwards. As George stepped up and inside, he heard low-level conversation, but he had to wait a moment for his eyes to adjust after leaving the bright sunlight outdoors.

He stood at the entrance to a large, open room. A counter ran partway across the left wall and ended at an open doorway at the rear. Rounded-top stools on metal posts stood in front of it. To his left was a single booth against the front wall. To his right were three more. Ahead of him stood a pool table flanked by four players. A couple of smaller tables stood along the right wall. A doorway passed through the back of the wall over there too. That one had a door and the door was closed.

He expected the place to be dirty, but the dust from the gravel driveway was filtered by the screen and only penetrated a few feet. The rest of the room was fairly clean.

A small, bald-headed man stood behind the counter looking at him. George glanced back at the four men shooting pool. They were in their thirties or forties and weathered looking. Three were standing like sentinels with the butt of their cue sticks on the floor, their sticks held upright by a fist near the tips. They were watching the fourth man line up for his shot.

As they stepped aside for the man to make his way around the table for the next shot, George noticed every one of them was carrying a handgun. Two were openly carrying in belt holsters and one had the grips protruding from his hip pocket. He couldn't see the gun on the man lining up his shot, but saw the weight of it sagging the chest pocket of his bib overalls.

The men glanced up as he entered, then immediately returned their attention to the game. George proceeded to the counter and swung his leg over a stool. It felt weird to turn his back on strangers with guns. It was quite different here compared to his former life in Vietnam where everyone had loaded guns. He knew he was going to have to make some mental adjustments here in the South. One of the adjustments was the heat and humidity. Without the acclimation from his tours in Vietnam, he doubted he would have stayed in this area.

The old man was friendly and openly inquisitive. "I ain't seen you in here before."

"You're right. I just came down to Portsmouth to visit a friend, but I like the area."

"Tidewater area. Whereabouts you from?"

"Originally Indiana, but I don't have a home there anymore. It just sort of dried up and blew away while I was in Service."

"You over there in China?"

"Vietnam, yes, twice. I was wounded the second time."

The old man mulled that over for a minute. "Bad stuff. A couple boys from around here ain't come home yet." He stuck out his hand. "I'm Pap!" Pap was browned and wizened looking, skin stretched over ropey muscles. His coloring belied his blue eyes and he looked a little like an older version of Henry from the comic strip.

They stared at each other for a moment and then shook hands. George said his name and asked for a cheeseburger deluxe.

"Deluxe?"

"Lettuce, tomato and mayonnaise—and a coke."

"What flavor?"

"Flavor?"

"What flavor coke?"

"Oh, regular coke, twelve-ounce."

George didn't act surprised at the different terminology, he just passed himself off as forgetful.

The old man hadn't written down a thing. "First burger and coke are on the house for a war veteran." He turned and disappeared through the door in back.

George swiveled around on his stool to see how the pool game was progressing. A different player was shooting now and two of the men were looking at George. One of them, the man with the bib overalls nodded at him. George nodded back and the two men returned their attention to the game. From their play, he knew he could have beaten any one of them. The Army provided in that regard, but he didn't make any attempt to challenge them.

George turned his attention to the sidewall at the front end of the counter. A mounted pegboard displayed an array of fishing tackle.

He stood up and walked over for a closer look while he was waiting. He decided to buy some tackle before he left.

When the old man returned with his meal, George asked him about fishing along the waterway.

"Lots of bullheads and eels. There's some decent catfish too, but you might catch anything. Even crabs." He laughed at his own wit and George laughed along with him. The pool players ignored it all.

George finished his burger and the fries that came with it, then said, "I'm going to add some tackle to the bill." He picked out some line, hooks, bobbers and sinkers.

"You're better off without the bobbers, just fish a foot or two off the bottom. You have a pole, or bait?"

"Neither."

"I have an old rod you can borry, and I've got bloodworms for sale in a cooler in back."

"You'd loan me a pole and you don't even know me?"

"Yes I do. You just told me your name."

"OK, I'll bring it back in a few days."

"How's about you catch 'em and clean 'em, and I'll cook 'em. We'll both eat 'em."

George grinned and shook hands with him. "Thanks Pap."

"Just don't bring me no eels. Give them to the Coloreds if you see any."

The pool shooters left a minute earlier and as George turned to leave, shots rang out BAM, BAM, BAM... from just outside the door. It momentarily jolted him. He turned to Pap with a questioning look.

"Somebody just shot a snake out by the door."

They stepped over and looked out. Two men stood there with revolvers in their hands. One held his other hand aloft and a dead rattler about four feet long dangled from it. Now George understood about the guns. He was back in enemy territory, the slithery kind.

* * *

George called Will that night but received no answer. He tried again the next morning and still didn't reach him, so he went fishing. It didn't take long to find out about the eels. As soon as he brought them to the surface, they would flop around in a frenzy and tangle his line into knots. He finally developed a strategy. As soon as he saw the eel, he would yank it out of the water, swing it in a fast arc over his head, and slam it onto the ground. While it was still stunned, he would step on it and remove his hook.

Just as he was leaving, an old Dodge pickup pulled in. Two older Negroes climbed out and began unloading their meager tackle.

George pointed over into the weeds. "There's three or four eels over there if you want them."

One man ran over with a bucket and gathered them up while the other thanked him profusely. Afterward, any time they saw his car parked along the waterway they would stop and check for eels.

George continued his occasional visits to Pap's and they became friends. On his third trip, they formed an even stronger bond. He was sitting at the counter eating his traditional cheeseburger when three young men came in dressed in casual clothes. From their dress and speech, he could tell they were not local. The most vocal one was about George's size and age. He was dark complexioned, with black wavy hair and a large thin nose. He looked Italian to George, but his companions could have been a mix of any Caucasian race. George thought of the vocal one as Rocky, thinking of Rocky Marciano.

The men looked like trouble, but they ordered cold-cut sandwiches and drinks to go, so George didn't pay them any more attention. They shot a game of cutthroat pool behind him while they waited, but George never turned around to watch. He just listened. Their talk was laced with profanity.

When their order was ready, they paid and one carried all of the food out in a grocery bag while another carried the canned drinks. The leader, the last one out, stopped just short of the door.

He addressed the old man. "Got any Hershey bars?"

"Male or female?"

"Huh! What's the difference?"

Pap burst our laughing. "The male has nuts." George laughed too.

"You think that's funny old man?" Rocky grabbed a sugar shaker from the nearby booth and flung it at Pap.

George jumped up from the stool and started toward him.

"Stay out of this, Hillbilly."

George didn't speak, he was moving fast, laughing to himself about the Hillbilly remark. He feinted with his left and his uppercut caught the man right under the chin. Rocky's feet left the floor and he landed flat on his back half-in and half-out of the door, unconscious.

The next man, shorter, stockier and lighter complexioned stepped back in through the screen door and over his buddy. A knife appeared in his right hand as if by magic. The switchblade swung open and clicked into place as George advanced. The man lunged at George's stomach and the knife snagged on his loose shirt.

George grabbed the man's right wrist with his own right hand and pushed it toward the man's own stomach. The man extended his arm to keep from getting cut and George grabbed his elbow with his other hand. With a yank upward and a twist, the knife nicked the man's forehead, and his shoulder popped. He let out a scream and the knife clattered to the floor.

The third man, standing in the doorway, caught the sugar shaker full in the face. He went down too. Pap stood at the end of the counter with an evil grin.

Rocky rose and stumbled out the door just as the third one was rising. They went down in a tangle. The one with the dislocated shoulder crawled over them and made his way out, cursing. They were like cartoon figures as they loaded into their Chevy convertible and rocketed out of the lot, spraying gravel as they fishtailed onto the highway heading north.

George scooped up the knife with a napkin and turned to Pap. "Here's his fingerprints, for the cops."

"Won't need it, you keep it. We already took care of them. They won't be back."

"That was a hell of a throw. Didn't you get hit?"

"No, I caught it. I used to pitch for the minors."

George laughed so hard he had to sit down. Later in the day he came back with some cleaned catfish. Pap cooked them and they both ate them. Pap's two sons were there but didn't share in the feast. George hadn't met the sons before, but they already knew about him and the run-in with the three city slickers.

Pap said, "George would have taken care of all three of 'em but I wanted to get in on it too. Man, that was something."

George knew he had established a reputation with the men of Dismal Swamp.

CHAPTER 21

Will

I HATED PUTTING GEORGE OFF AFTER BRINGING HIM DOWN HERE, but I had things to do. There had to be a way to get a line on Bustamonte and therefore a path to his money. I needed to restore the Howell money and have my expenses covered or our efforts would be wasted. I questioned Murta again.

She said, "He spends far more time ashore than he does on the yacht. Where he goes? I do not know. That is why I was so surprised to see him in the restaurant."

"Did he see you?"

"No, or his men would have come after me right then."

"Well, maybe not. The place is too public."

She shook her head no, and I hoped she was wrong. Surely they wouldn't be that bold. She and Marisol were already feeling confined, even though they were not prisoners. They felt being dependent on me, a stranger, also kept them from seeking asylum elsewhere. She readily admitted though, Bustamonte had large tentacles spread over many cities. How far and how many remained to be seen.

She said, "Bustamonte has a brother named Ji who travels with him sometimes. I overheard crew members saying Ji is very cruel. They refer to him as Bustamonte's torture man. I have never seen him.

"There is also a man named Adolfo, next in command, reporting only to Bustamonte himself. It is said Adolfo has many freedoms and first choice of captives when Bustamonte isn't interested or is tired of them.

"Adolfo put his hands all over me and said it wouldn't be long before I was his."

I started my search that afternoon by cruising the area of the restaurant where I met Murta and Marisol. I also decided to begin eating there in hopes Bustamonte would come back. I thought of taking Nina there on a date, but immediately thought against it. If they showed up and saw her, they would want her too. Or, if they saw me as an enemy, they might use her to get at me.

Nina was on my mind, so when I noticed a phone booth, I called her and made a date with her. I felt like a schoolboy, asking her if she would like to go to a dinner and a movie.

She said she would, that evening. My search for Bustamonte would have to wait.

The date went well although things proceeded slowly at first, feeling each other out. This was different from our business meeting before, but things smoothed out and we relaxed. I could tell I would have to go slowly with this woman. Her primary clothing colors were red and black, or black and white. They complimented her flashing dark eyes, golden skin, beautiful, straight white teeth and red lipstick. If I wasn't careful, I'd be hooked.

For the next few days, I continued prowling the area around Mateo's restaurant, occasionally eating there, hoping Bustamonte had a business office nearby and that I would spot him. Murta told me that he was tall and handsome with short, wavy black hair and "eyes as blue as the sea." She said he had strong, rugged features and an olive complexion. I could tell he had impressed her. Things changed when she found out who and what he was. But by then it was too late. They were already taken.

I wished I had brought George into the whole picture so he could help me search. Finding out what I was up against first had more appeal. Besides, George needed time to become acclimated to the area, time to take care of his personal business. I was glad to hear he was acting on his own initiative and was buying the two cars, but then I expected nothing less from him.

I knew George pretty well but I needed to know him even better, including his fighting, handgun-shooting skills and skills with other weapons. I had no doubts about his skill with a rifle. There were other important skills too. Could he keep his mouth shut? Could he work with others even if he didn't like them? Could he follow orders if they became necessary? Could he kill, and would he kill only those necessary to kill? How did he react to women and children, and toward other races? I intended to find out as soon as possible.

The third night, after George and I talked on the phone, I drove over to Webster Avenue. Both cars were parked at the curb, the Ford with a new Virginia license plate. The Chevy had only a paper taped to the inside of the back window. I walked over and looked, but it was only a bill-of-sale. George wasn't home, so I just returned to my car and waited. It was getting close to dark when I saw him coming along the sidewalk in my mirror. I didn't think he'd noticed me so I slumped down and eased over to the passenger side.

When I could tell by his footsteps that he was close, I swung the door open and rolled out. He was right there in front of me with his left hand extended from the hip with a pointing-gun gesture. I saw his teeth flash in a grin.

"Howdy Will. I've been expecting you."

I rose and laughed with him. "Were you just out walking?"

"I was over to the "Y" working out. Right now I'm having some pain in my back and side. Come on in and have a beer."

As we entered, I asked him if it was from the war wound.

"Yes, but it's getting better. How about your back?"

"The back is OK but I had a cracked vertebrae the military doctors never told me about. It's healed now. I see a chiropractor occasionally. It works."

"Man, I'll never forget the look on your face when I pulled your pants down!"

We both laughed about the incident. When he returned with the beers, we sat down and clinked bottles.

"Tell me about the "Y", what are you doing there?"

"Mostly weights, a rowing machine and a bicycle up on a stand. They don't have any mats or bags."

"We need to find a decent gym so we can both work out, hone our skills. Working together, we need to know each other's capabilities. We can probably strengthen each other's skills."

"I'm up for it, you look a little soft, Will."

I grinned back at him and told him about the two Negroes.

"Wait a minute! What woman? What little girl? Are you shacked up?"

I laughed again. "No, they're my tenants, my neighbors."

"Sounds like 'close neighbors' to me." Then he proceeded to tell me about the three city boys in a place called Pap's.

We got down to the nitty gritty and I told him about the Howells, Cletus Arnold, Murta, and Bustamonte. Afterward, I said, "Why don't you come over tomorrow afternoon and see where I live. You can meet Murta and Marisol and hear their story. I bought a charcoal grill. We can burn some burgers and dogs."

"I need to bring something, how about beer and pop?"

We agreed on the visit, and on a time. George said he would find a gym in Norfolk where we could work out.

I left thinking about Nina. I would have liked to invite her to the cookout, but I wasn't sure how she would react to Murta living on the other side of the wall. Instead, I invited Nina to go on a picnic. I knew I had to postpone the cookout to the following weekend, so I turned around and went back and told George.

He flashed me his big grin. "Good luck with your date."

* * *

Nina agreed and we decided to make it a beach picnic at Virginia Beach. I drove down as close to the water as I could without getting stuck in the sand, and we walked the rest of the way. I took soft drinks and a bottle of white wine the clerk at the Alcoholic Beverage Control (ABC) store assured me was a good choice, packed in a Styrofoam cooler. She brought potato salad and fried chicken for me and eight or nine Mexican rollups for both of us.

I was pretty sure she'd bought the chicken and potato salad, but she'd made the Mexican dishes herself. Two of them were desserts. Her rollups were so good we ate them all and I only ate one piece of chicken.

My main interest was seeing her in a bathing suit, and I wasn't disappointed. She was wearing a red and green floral print, just-below-the-knee garment that looked to me like a cross between a kimono and a housecoat. The garment buttoned down the front and I complimented her on it. She told me it was a beach robe.

She was also wearing leather sandals and I noticed she had painted her toenails the same bright red as her lips. I would have kissed them both. Once we were situated on the blanket, she kicked her sandals off and sat sideways. I got glimpses of her legs as we ate and I could tell by the smile she knew I was admiring her.

We passed the time with small talk until after we ate. She packed everything back into the basket she'd brought and pushed it aside. I was ready to rip the robe from her body, but thought of other things to keep from becoming obvious. I was wearing Bermuda shorts over my trunks, along with a Hawaiian shirt and sneakers.

Nina said, "It's too soon after eating to swim. We'll get cramps." I didn't mention all of my years of swimming in Florida. Then she laid back and pulled on my supporting arm forcing me to lie down beside her.

She was on her left side facing me and I lay halfway between my back and my side. Before I knew what she was up to, she reached over and cupped the side of my face. Then she pulled my head toward hers and planted a slow, soft kiss on my cheek.

"Thank you for being a gentleman, Will."

A gentleman was the last thing I wanted to be. I rolled on over facing her and lightly smoothed the hair away from her face. Her eyes were deep, dark-liquid, bottomless pools and I fell into them.

I was the one forced to break away from our first kiss. It was so soft, so sweet and so wonderful without being wildly passionate.

Women have a big advantage. Their bodies don't betray them the way a man's does. I should have been wearing two jock straps under my shorts and trunks.

We both rolled away onto our backs and I pulled my knees up. It occurred to me there were other people around us, within fifty feet. Nina reached over and worked her fingers under the back of my neck and we just lay there for a while, not speaking.

Finally, she rolled over onto her hands and knees and rose to a kneeling position. "I think we can go in the water now."

She started unbuttoning her robe and I sat up and wrapped my arms around my knees, watching. She wore a two-piece like I had never seen before. It wasn't a string bikini, but wasn't far from it either. It was white and dotted with little red and black fishes with curled-up tails and pursed lips. Some of the fish were red and some black, and some both colors. I could see too much flesh and had to tear my eyes away. Her figure was stunning. I thought back to when she said the other woman had "big bazooms," and laughed to myself. Nina's breasts were perfect. I couldn't help but think back to Eva's. They were the same in my mind's eye although Eve's body was lither.

As Nina stood, she reached over and slapped me lightly on the cheek. "Come on. You do have a swimming suit under those Bermuda shorts, don't you?"

No answer was needed as I nearly tore the buttons off my shirt getting out of it. By the time I stood and reached to pull down my shorts she was already turned away, toward the water.

We had a barrel of fun playing in the sand and water that day and I hated to see it end. I suspected she wasn't going to let me in when I took her home, and I was right. I did get to keep the rest of the chicken and the potato salad, though. The real highlight to the day was the goodnight kiss.

CHAPTER 22

It was still June, not too hot to sit in a car and watch, and after nearly a week, my vigilance paid off. Friday, right at noon, I spotted Bustamonte and three other men walking into Mateo's restaurant. It wasn't hard to figure out which one was Ji. The Ji must have come from Giant. He was a monster, over seven feet tall——and solid. His head was as large as a peck basket. Massive arms hung down nearly to his knees. He braced himself against the doorframe with a hand as large as a country ham as he ducked and squatted to get through it. His thumb and fingers gripped both sides of the wall. His face looked like it had been worked over with a meat tenderizer and it hadn't taken.

Despite it all, he still looked like his brother, the boss, Bustamonte. I found out later that Ji's full name was Gigantesco.

I found a parking place not far away and walked back to the restaurant. The four of them sat at the same table as before and the hostess walked me past them to a table. Only one glanced my way, a tall, thin, hatchet-faced Latin with a hooked nose and a wide, thin mustache. I didn't want to call attention to myself by asking for a specific location, so I kept my mouth shut and my eyes on the rear of the hostess leading me toward where I was seated before. I didn't get the same table as before, but it was still in a good spot. I couldn't see them and they couldn't see me. Unfortunately, I couldn't hear them either.

Later, when they left, the thin man glanced quickly around the corner, not letting his gaze rest on anyone.

I lingered over a dessert and when the plump, blonde waitress with a worn-out look brought my bill, I asked who the important looking man in the tan slacks and white shirt was.

She gave me an appraising look. "That's Mister Bustamonte. We don't talk about our regular customers."

I thanked her without comment and left her a good, but not excessive, tip.

I was surprised when I reached the door and saw them standing just outside and to the right. I stayed inside and watched through the window as a white, stretched Lincoln picked them up. None of them looked my way, so when it left I hot-footed over to my Studebaker and followed a full block-and-a-half behind. They didn't go far.

When the limo stopped, I stopped also and turned into an alley. The timing was right and I saw them exiting in front of a large, modern four-story building. I drove around randomly for fifteen minutes before driving by the front of the building. Carved into the stone header above the door, in block letters, was the name TESCO. It could be useful information.

* * *

Sunday, the day of the cookout, George was already there, sitting in his Ford in front of the duplex when I arrived. I saw a glimpse of a face on the B-side and knew Murta was keeping an eye out. I hadn't told her George was coming. They were probably scared.

I took George on through, and we grabbed meat, charcoal and drinks along the way. Then we went back, carried my table through, and followed it with the chairs. The furniture was just one of the things occupying my time during the past few days. Groceries for both sides was another, although Murta and Marisol went with me for the food. Earlier, I told Murta we were going to have a cookout, so she was preparing the balance of the food.

When George and I were ready, I knocked on Murta's back door. I saw the surprised look on her face when she saw George. I glanced at him and saw his surprise too. Oh, oh, there was a spark there, something I hadn't expected. I believed Murta was five-to-ten years older than George. Still, she was a beautiful woman.

George looked down at Marisol and gave her his big white grin. "Hi Sugar. You sure are a beautiful girl."

Marisol actually blushed. "Thank you, sir."

I glanced at Murta to see her response... a big smile.

George reached out and briefly shook Marisol's hand before shaking Murta's. That shake lingered, but Murta didn't blush. Instead, without taking her eyes from George, she said, "I'll go get another chair. I see that you only have three."

When she left, George said, "You didn't tell me."

I just shrugged and said, "Oh well." It was time for me to grill, so I fired it up while they got acquainted. By the time the meat was ready they were friends.

When we sat down to eat, Murta said, "Someone is knocking on your door."

I set down my spatula. "Murta, you and Marisol had better go inside." She grabbed Marisol's hand without question and left.

Without saying a word, George followed me back inside and took a position behind the door before I opened it. I liked the backup. I was still surprised when I opened it. Standing in front of my door was the redbone who tried to sucker punch me, along with a woman and a little girl.

He just stood there for a moment with a flustered look on his face. "Go ahead," the woman said. For the first time I noticed she was holding a vase of mixed flowers.

The man said, "My name's Lavon Goodson. I came down to apologize to you and the little girl."

I just looked at him for a moment and he held my gaze. "Apology accepted. Thank you."

George stepped around me and looked out at them. Then he stepped halfway in front of me, stuck his hand out and said, "I'm George."

Lavon took a step back when George appeared in front of me, but now he stepped back up and took George's hand. "You look tougher'n the other one, and he was bad enough."

We all laughed. The doorway was getting crowded so I pushed George on out, followed him, and stuck out my hand. "I'm Will, Lavon, and who is this?"

"This be my wife Ernestine and our daughter Chloe."

George and I exchanged looks. I thought, what the hell, so I invited them to join us for the cookout.

The woman said "Yes we will," before Lavon had a chance to speak. They followed us on through my house like a parade. When we reached the outside, I knocked on Murta's back door again.

"Murta, we need three more chairs."

When she opened the door, George stepped up and said, "I'll help with the chairs."

After the introductions, Chloe handed the flowers to Marisol. Ernestine said, "You ain't got enough for all of us. I need to run down and get something."

She left and returned in a few minutes with some pork barbeque and some more buns.

While she was gone, Lavon said, "We thought Murta was your wife."

I let Murta handle that one. "No, we are friends and we needed a place to stay, so Will is helping us out."

I could see him working it around in his head so I said, "Lavon, Murta is hiding from a very bad man named Buster. I thought you might be one of his men."

"I wouldn't work for no one who would go after women and children."

We let the subject drop and turned to other topics. Eventually, we worked it out that Lavon would take care of the yard work for the duplex at two dollars an hour. He seemed glad to have the opportunity and said, "Thank you. Minimum wage is a dollar an hour and that's all we getting. Nobody pays overtime, even if you work it. They don't pay extra for holidays neither, and I work most of 'em doing this or that."

He'd already told me he worked on the city garbage pickup, so I knew he wasn't making much money. With Ernestine's barbeque added to the food, we wound up with a good cookout. The Goodsons left early, possibly sensing we wanted the privacy, and thanked us for inviting them.

After they left, I told George and Murta about the men I saw, and where they went. She said the thin man was Adolfo, as I expected. She didn't know who the other man was from the description. The man was medium height with thinning gray hair. He was wearing a decent suit, but was wearing white socks with it. We agreed it didn't fit with Bustamonte's crowd. She didn't know anything about the building.

It was late before everyone left except George. He said, "Will, you can't be driving around down there anymore in the Studebaker. They may have already spotted you. Why don't you ride back with me, then you can bring the Chevy over here. Next week we will switch off hunting them down."

I concurred and brought the Chevy home. I also paid him for it. The next day, I registered it with a bogus Norfolk address. The following night, I picked up George and drove through Norfolk and on out to the airport. In long-term parking, we stole license plates from four cars similar to ours. Two for the Chevy and two for the Ford.

After midnight, from different areas, we swapped the stolen plates with others from the same make, model and colors. Now the only cars with missing plates were in Long Term Parking and none of theirs were on our cars.

We resumed our search for Bustamonte on a Tuesday, using the two-tone Chevy with the bogus plates. George drove alone one day and I drove the next. The following Monday evening, about six o'clock, I spotted the Brazilians again. The Lincoln drove out to a huge car dealership on the outskirts of Norfolk. It covered several acres, the largest I had ever seen. Bustamonte's limo motored slowly back and forth through the lanes of cars and I was forced to park in the used car lot and dodge salesmen who headed toward me from different directions like frogs in a pond after a crippled minnow.

I lost sight of the Lincoln for a few minutes, but then it headed back out as if they gave up looking for a car. They led me back into the city where the traffic was thick, intermittent stop-and-go. It was hard to keep them in sight and my attention was focused on the glimpse of white roof up ahead. I was stopped with my head halfway out of the driver's side window when the passenger-side door opened and a man slid onto the seat.

The man was Adolfo and he held a large revolver down at his waist, pointed at my guts. "Keep following the white Lincoln Mister. Work your way up behind it."

A hundred thoughts ran through my mind. The first was that I had made a rank, amateur mistake. As soon as that sunk in, I realized I made a number of them. I should have had George following me as backup too. My mind kept churning while I followed his commands. If we hadn't switched to the Chevy and used false plates, the car would have led them right back to Murta. Escape raced through my thoughts too. I looked for an opening where I could bail out and take my chances on being shot or run over, but soon realized another car was behind me, right on my bumper. In the mirror, I saw three or four heads through the windshield. Shit!

CHAPTER 23

THE THOUGHTS CAME CRASHING HOME. MY LIFE WAS HANGING BY A thread.

"Who are you? Why are you spying on us?"

This guy was good, a real pro. His English was Midwest American. I racked my brain for an answer. If I didn't give him something believable, he would know it.

"Cletus Arnold. He owed me money!"

"Not good enough." His eyes flicked to the rear, the car behind us. I glanced in the side mirror and he cracked me on the side of the head with the pistol barrel.

It hurt like hell but I kept the car straight. I hit the brakes and the car behind us slammed into us and knocked us forward. Adolfo's head bounced back and shot forward. My timing was right-on and I caught him on the chin with a backhand fist as he came forward.

The blow stunned him and I grabbed the gun with my right hand. He didn't relinquish his grip though. We struggled for it while I was still trying to keep the car pointed straight.

His left hand dipped behind his neck and came out with a dagger. I barely saw it before he sunk the point of it into the side of my neck.

My struggle was over and I let go of the pistol.

He yanked the dagger out. It felt like two inches deep, but I saw blood only on the first half-inch or so.

"You see Mister. You are overmatched."

I just nodded. I had no comeback for that.

"Tough guy huh? What's your name tough guy?"

"Real," I blurted.

"Well Mister Real, before this day is over, you will tell us everything we want to know and many things we have no interest in.

* * *

Our little parade circled around Norfolk and crossed back over the highway leading to the tunnel back to Portsmouth. I could feel the blood seeping into my shirt while I drove, but tried to keep my mind focused on my surroundings. He sat stoically beside me, dagger in one hand, gun in the other.

We left the residential area and entered a conglomeration of railroad tracks and warehouses, still on the Norfolk side. Finally, we stopped between two rows of seemingly deserted warehouses, out of sight of traffic.

"Do not move. They will come and get you. Gigantesco will pull answers from you like pulling teeth from a child."

After thoroughly frisking me and failing to find a wallet or weapons, three men marched me into a warehouse and up an open, grated-steel stairway to a high second floor. Along the way, I saw the tattoo Cynthia Leggit described, and memorized the man's features. His head was rectangular, he had a crooked nose, his eyes were too close together and his hairline was a widow's peak. He did have strong hands too. I felt the strength when he dug his thumb into my arm looking for a nerve. It wasn't easy but I ignored it.

Adolfo followed along with his revolver and his dagger. Along the way, he wiped the dagger clean on my shirt and put it away. They shoved me through a doorway and slammed the door shut behind me.

I was in an open room at least fifty yards long and half that wide with four columns spaced apart in the center over the length of it. The room contained four wooden kitchen chairs and two men. Three of the chairs sat in a row facing the fourth. Ji sat on two of the chairs while Bustamonte sat on the third. The facing chair was left to me.

Ji just grinned at me with big, widely spaced teeth. He kneaded his hands together like he couldn't wait to get started. His big, bulging brown eyes were three inches apart.

Bustamonte did the talking. "Welcome Mister Real. Have a seat. Now I want to know who you are and what you expected to get from us. If you don't tell me, Ji will start by breaking your fingers one-by-one. Then he will start on larger bones. He can tear a man's limbs completely off once he breaks the joint. He bites into it to get it started. But you may not last that long."

I knew they would kill me anyway. "FUCK YOU!"

His face purple, Bustamonte rose. Ignoring me, he said, "He's all yours, Ji." With four knocks, the door opened and Bustamonte left. It slammed shut behind him and I was alone with the giant.

I did what any tough guy would do. I ran like hell!

I snatched up the chair meant for me, and then a second one as I dodged around him. He was incredibly fast and it didn't bother him in the least that I had the chairs for weapons.

I tossed one chair in his path and his huge foot went through the rungs, tripping him and breaking the chair. He went down on his face with a grunt, and emitted childish curses. From what I heard, he wasn't much above idiot level.

I smashed the seat of the other chair against his skull and it was like hitting a brick wall. He squealed and when I swung it for a second blow, he ripped it from my hands and smashed it to pieces on the floor. I nearly fell into his range before I thought to let go. I ran for the other two chairs as he staggered to his feet. Blood oozed down the side of his head and dribbled around his pig-sized ear, but he ignored it. He was probably used to banging his head.

He was more cautious in his approach this time.

I swung one of the chairs at his head, hoping he would grab at it with both hands.

He did.

I leaped forward with the other chair and rammed the legs into his guts, trying for his groin.

He went down bleating like a sheep, but only to a sitting position, one chair still in his grasp. He swung it in an arc and knocked me off my feet.

I rolled with it and was back on my feet instantly. I hadn't lost my grip on the other chair, but it was the only one left, and he had one too. Before he could get back up, I ran again.

I reached an outside wall and used the chair to break out a window glass. The windows were up high and only half height. I knew it was a long ways down on the outside, but I would take the chance. Learning to drop from upper floors was part of escape and evasion training.

Ji cast the chair aside and was back on his feet. He was almost to me when I made it through. The chair thrust slowed him just enough.

He poked his head through the window, looking for me, and I was ready for him. My luck had turned, if only momentarily. There was a six-inch-deep concrete windowsill and a heavy downspout ran alongside the window. I managed to grab it and pull myself up when I went through.

While his chin was still above the windowsill, I stomped down as hard as I could. I went for the sweet spot at the base of the skull. I didn't know if it killed him or not, so I just kept kicking him in the head and stomping on the back of the neck until I felt the drainpipe starting to loosen. Dark blood was oozing out of his ears and one eye. I grabbed him by the hair and tried to pull him on through so he would hit the pavement below, but his weight was too much for me to handle. Instead, I pushed him back inside with my foot.

As I slid on down the pipe, I realized if I had pulled him through, the others would have probably heard the impact when he hit.

When I reached the ground, I scrambled around the building on all fours so I was below the windows. When I peered around the corner to where the cars were, I saw that my Chevy and their Lincoln were still there, but the car that had been following behind me was gone.

The only man around was the driver of the limo, and he was stretched out asleep behind the wheel. He was about my size, with tanned skin and short, dyed-blond hair. I eased past the Chevy and noticed the keys were still in the ignition. I looked around and found a fist–sized rock someone had been using as a door chock. I yanked the car door open and grabbed the driver by the hair to pull him out. He helped by hanging onto the car with both hands to resist the pull.

The rock impacted his left temple with a solid smack. I took his keys and wallet. And then I found the big prize. He was wearing a shoulder rig with a .45 auto in it. I wrestled his tan sports coat off and took it along with the gun and holster. A full, spare magazine was in the left outside coat pocket. There was no time to waste, so I dropped it into my shirt pocket.

Thinking about what George had done to me in the helicopter flashed through my mind. Sparing a few seconds, and for a slap in the face to all of them, I yanked off his loafers and removed his pants and undershorts. I propped him back behind the wheel where I'd found him——bottomless. He was still breathing when I left, but I doubted he would be much good to anyone after this. I took the clothes and shoes with me. I thought about the shirt, but his was bloody too.

I threw the clothes and holster onto the passenger seat of the Chevy and checked the pistol. It was a standard Army issue Model 1911 in good shape. I peered down the barrel and saw the copper jacket looking back at me, then popped the magazine free and checked the count. It held a full seven rounds.

It took me a few minutes to get my bearings, but before long I knew where I was. Even better, I would be able to find my way back. After learning what they planned for me, I held no compunctions about killing any of them. I kept the sports coat but dumped the rest of the clothes into a trash dumpster behind a Sears store.

It was late when I arrived back in Portsmouth, around 9 o'clock, but George was sitting out on the porch in the dark. I was glad of it because I remembered his medical skills. My neck stiffened up and it was hurting like hell. He waved me to a seat but I motioned for him to come inside with me. He caught on and followed without saying anything.

I headed straight for the bathroom and started easing out of my shirt. He followed and gripped my shoulder so he could get a good look.

"Jesus, you do get around. What the hell happened?"

"Got anything stronger than beer?"

"I have some vodka, but it may not be strong enough. You're going to need a couple stitches. How deep is it anyway?"

"About an inch."

"Move your head all around."

I had full range of motion, it was just sore.

"Tell me about it while you're getting soused."

So I told him the story and showed him the .45 while I drank some of the vodka straight, with a beer chaser. I didn't care for it that way, but I knew what was coming.

He flushed my wound with hydrogen peroxide and sewed me up with tan thread from his little sewing kit. I chewed on a dishtowel while he was doing it and it still hurt like a bastard. When he finished, I crashed on his sofa, something new since I'd been there last.

The next morning, George said, "We're going to have to lose the Chevy. It's traceable right back to both of us. We need some new wheels."

"Yes, and a stock of medical supplies. I know where I can get the stuff we can't buy in a drug store."

"Oh?"

"Howell, the Marine who brought me here to start with. He's in rehab less than half a mile from here. He can get it from the Naval Hospital."

"Good, and I know how to get us a couple more cars. Driving around in the country, I see them sitting along the road for sale. People don't check ID's if you have cash. I think I can get someone to help, for a price."

"Oh, who?"

"A colored guy I met not far from here, a Korean War Veteran."

"That's good. Bustamonte wouldn't link a Negro to me or Murta."

"Speaking of her, do you have something going there?"

Now I felt like teasing him a little. "Nah, she's way too old for either of us. Not bad looking though."

"Huh, that just goes to show what little you know. Most of the women I've been with, and the best of them, have been older than me."

"I'm just pulling your chain. Actually, I have someone I'm seeing in case you've forgotten. I just didn't think it would be a good idea to bring her around Murta."

"Probably not."

We sat for a few minutes drinking beer and George said, "Something else. They know you're after them and for sure they will launch a big campaign to find you. We're going to need more firepower. I know some people out in the country. I'll see what I can do."

"Good. Do you need money?

"Not up front, but we should keep some on hand. Are you running short?"

"No, I have a stash and a couple bank accounts. I'll get you a thousand in a couple days."

After the conversation, George drove me back to my duplex. He left me the Ford and took my Studebaker home. He said he'd find a way to get rid of the Chevy.

I spent some time working on a plan after I finished appeasing Murta. It didn't take long for her to spot the bandage when I came in, even though it was dark.

Certain a man couldn't deal with something like injuries, she removed the bandage and examined the wound. Afterward, she was satisfied.

"Who did this? You should stop this fighting before they kill you."

"George sowed it up, but we weren't fighting." She scowled at me, so I continued. "I had a run-in with Adolfo and his goons. He won this round and would have killed me, but I got away."

"Stop! Take me to another city where I can make a new life. I will send you money when I can. I am so afraid for Marisol."

She had a good point, and it would make things easier if we didn't have to worry about them.

"Listen, today is Monday. I will take you to Richmond in the morning and give you enough money to take a bus to somewhere else. You should be able to get settled in by the weekend. I don't want to know where you wind up, OK? Don't mail me anything. It would be traceable."

"Yes. That is safer, but how will I repay you."

I smiled at her. "When you get settled, write to George. He has a Post Office box."

She seemed to like the idea.

The next morning, I made a run to the bank while they were packing their clothes. Before the day was over, I dropped them off at the Greyhound station in Richmond and was back in Craddock.

George was disappointed they were gone, but agreed it was safer for all of us. He perked up when I told him she would write to him. The following morning, I called and placed orders for phone installations at George's apartment on Webster Avenue and in the empty, B-side of the duplex, both numbers unlisted.

CHAPTER 24

George

GEORGE DROVE THE CHEVY DOWN TO PAP'S TRUCK STOP AND PARKED it around behind the building. He saw Pap watching him with a quizzical look from the back door. George waved and walked back around. He entered through the front, even though no one else was there.

"Pap, I need a favor, actually a couple, but I can pay."

"What's going on, George?"

"My friend Will got tangled up with a gang in Norfolk, some real bad-asses. We need to hide this car for a couple weeks. They'll be looking for it, but I doubt they'll come way out here."

"We can take it into Dismal. Nobody will ever find it back in there," Pap offered.

"Good. The sooner the better."

"Now what's the other thing?"

"Well, I need some snake protection too, and a deer rifle."

"Deer rifle! You need deer protection too? The huntin' season don't even open for three months."

"I'll need to practice with it."

George just waited while Pap thought it over. He knew Pap was pulling his leg, and after a moment decided to tell him some of it.

"Look, Pap, these guys are kidnapping women and kids, turning them into sex slaves and working them in mines in South America. Will just happened to be in their way of a kidnapping, and rescued a woman and a little girl."

"Bad stuff. I've heard of women and kids going missing out around Virginia Beach. What's this character's name?"

"Bustamonte. He's a Brazilian."

"Never heard of him. At least he's not from around here." He thought for a moment. "Lester, my oldest boy, is going to be here in a few minutes. He can probably get you anything you want."

Lester turned out to be one of the pool players, the guy with bib overalls George noticed during his first stop at Pap's.

After the introductions, Lester said, "You want to foller me in your car. We can run you back up to Portsmouth afterward."

Lester loaded a small aluminum jon boat, propped up against the back wall of the store, into the bed of his pickup and drove north along the highway. A few miles farther, he pulled off into a stop George had been to before——the deserted dock.

George helped him slide the boat down the bank to the canal. Halfway down, Lester killed a water moccasin with his paddle. He said, "Most of this canal was dug by slaves. Imagine the hell and the snakebites they went through. There's probably hundreds of men buried in the banks between here and Florida." Afterward, he said, "You stay here, I'll bring the barge back over and you just drive your car up onto it when I wave."

George gave him a thumbs-up. In a few minutes, he saw Lester uncovering a small outboard on one side of the barge. In a few more minutes, the barge was zigzagging back to his side of the canal.

Lester waved as he kept the barge powered up against the dock with the outboard. It seemed like a shaky operation to George. The barge tried to move away as the front end of the Chevy dropped down onto it, but Lester held it steady and George didn't hesitate.

When they reached the other side, Lester told him to tie it off before he shut the outboard down. "Leave a foot of slack on each rope so the barge can rise when you drive off."

After George drove off, Lester lengthened the slack to three feet on each end before he covered the outboard. As they drove the Chevy back into the swamp, Lester asked, "Ever been back in the Great Dismal before?"

"No, but I've been someplace similar."

"Vietnam?"

"Yeah."

"My best friend's boy went over there. Came back in a casket."

George just nodded. There was nothing to say that would make anyone feel better.

They drove back into the swamp for three-quarters of a mile and locked up the car. George removed the license plate and took it back with him. As they hiked back, he handed Lester the keys.

While they were walking, Lester spoke again. "They's a big lake back in here, Lake Drummond. If you ever go back in there to it, don't go swimmin'. You'll have cottonmouths hanging all over you." George knew the local wisdom was well worth listening to.

Lester drove him back into Portsmouth. Will's place was closest so George directed him there. He told Lester he would like to buy an Army .45 and maybe a couple of smaller pocket guns in good condition too. For a deer rifle, either a .270 or a .30-06 would do. They agreed on a price range and George gave him fifty dollars for hiding the Chevy and the ride to Portsmouth.

Will had just returned from Richmond, so George introduced him to Lester saying, "There will be another fifty when we pick the car up. If we're not back for it in a month, you can keep it. The papers are in the glove compartment."

Will concurred.

George drove around Norfolk in his Ford for a few days, scouting the area around the restaurant where it all started and down by the warehouses, without getting away from other traffic. More than once, he saw cars with three or four Hispanic looking men cruising the streets, heads swiveling in every direction. Each time he saw them he left the area. He didn't want to become conspicuous. He hadn't spotted any in Portsmouth yet, but it wouldn't surprise him if they expanded their search. He decided to work it out with Will so they could alternate cars. Then he remembered he was supposed to be finding a couple more cars.

The next day he went walking in the area where he met Alphonse, the Korean War veteran. Once he found someone to ask, Alphonse showed up in about thirty minutes.

"Oh, George. They just told me a white man was waiting for me by the water fountain. What's up, man?"

"I would like to hire you to go around with me and buy a couple of used cars from private owners."

"You need me for that?"

"Well, I don't know the best places to look. You might be able to make a better deal, depending on what we find. And I'll need someone to help me drive them to different spots. Plus, I'll be carrying cash, so having backup won't hurt."

"I get it. When do we start?"

"Right now if you're up to it. Tomorrow morning if you're not."

"You just gave me an excuse to leave the game money ahead. I'm ready if the money's right."

They struck a deal and went car shopping. The first one they bought was a 1958 Oldsmobile 98, green over white, from a colored woman school teacher in her fifties. The car was clean but had been rear-ended. The bumper and trunk lid were dented and the frame was bent slightly behind the rear axle, but it ran and drove OK. The trunk opened and closed and it still locked. George found that its 371 cubic inch engine had far more horsepower than his Ford's 312. They drove it out to Craddock and left it behind the A-side of Will's duplex.

The next morning, they found a white, 1960 Ford Falcon with a 144 cubic inch six-cylinder engine and automatic transmission. An older, white man owned it and he wouldn't deal with Alphonse. George intended to pay him his asking price, but the man's attitude ticked George off, so he wouldn't go higher than fifty dollars less. After striking the deal, but before they left, George gave the fifty to Alphonse as a bonus right in front of the man.

George said, "This man is a Korean War veteran who put his life on the line for this country."

The man remained grimfaced and silent, but Alphonse just laughed. He was used to hearing shit from white people.

They parked the Falcon on Webster Avenue, half-a-block from George's apartment.

Afterward, George said, "We'll let that old fart pay for his own prejudices."

"You're alright George. You see what we mean by nothings going to change anytime soon."

Afterward, George paid him off and invited him in for a beer. "We have enough cars for now, but I might need a driver again."

Alphonse grinned at him. "You have some kind of big deal going on, don't you? You ain't going to be robbing no banks, are you?"

"Not hardly. A friend is on the wrong side of some real bad-asses. There's a bunch of them. We're just trying to level the playing field. No crimes against the public."

"There's got to be some money in it too, or you wouldn't be laying out all this bread."

George looked at Alphonse with new eyes. "We think there's money, yes. There's no guarantee though."

"I want in on it, man. I was a forward observer in Korea. I have other points too, and I need the money."

"You're good with me, but I'll have to talk it over with Will first."

They shook on it and George promised to get back with him in a day or two.

* * *

George was restless. He didn't mind living alone, but he wanted a woman once in a while. He thought he might have a relationship with Murta, but Murta was gone before it could happen. He decided to check out the local bars, even though he wasn't a bar person. He quickly found out the local bars were filled with mostly sailors.

There were women too, and some of them good looking, but most of them were looking for a long-term relationship with the sailors.

For the most part, the sailors were either drunk and quarrelsome, or drunk and boisterous. George didn't doubt they were confined aboard ship for too long. George avoided getting into disputes with them and ignored the occasional shoulder bumps or beer sloshed onto his hands or shoes.

It didn't take long for a woman to find him though. She was older than most of the sailors and looked like she'd suffered a few hard knocks of her own. Still, she was fading-pretty, clean and sober.

She settled in at a stool next to George when its previous occupant left and gave him an appraising look. "Do you smoke?"

"No, I never have."

"Me neither," she responded. "It's hard to find anyone who doesn't, especially in here."

"I agree." George gave her an appraising look of his own. Her hair and teeth were clean, but her nails were bitten down to the quick. Her fingers were faded and wrinkled as if immersed in water for long periods. The dark brown hair was shoulder length, and not professionally cut. She hadn't ordered yet and the bartender was waiting.

"My name is George. Can I buy you a drink?"

"I'll drink beer or wine."

"Give the lady whatever she wants," he told the bartender.

After the bartender left with the order, she said, "Thank you. My name is Mona. I just got off from work down the street."

He didn't ask where, the area was full of bars and greasy spoons. Instead, he said, "What are you doing in here, Mona?"

"I'm just not ready to go home and stare at the walls until I fall asleep. What about you? Are you married?"

George laughed. "No, I've never done that either. I do like women though. Mostly what's in here are girls—looking for boys."

They clinked glass to that, her wine glass and his bottle. Later, they left and went to her apartment over a restaurant, where George spent the night. He was surprised at how good she was in bed, without being overeager. It was a need-fulfilling night for both of them. He left before she awoke the next morning.

Three nights later, George was back in the same bar, but Mona never showed up. He sipped his beer ignoring the cacophony around him for most of the evening. Suddenly, the noise rose to a crescendo. The argument was between a small man around thirty in civilian clothes and three larger, young sailors wearing whites.

George didn't catch the first part of the conversation, but he heard the biggest of the sailors say. "Tough shit, Runt."

In an instant the big sailor was down, curled up on his side, gasping for breath. Another of the three spoke up. "Fucking Seals are midgets with attitudes." And then he was down too, clutching his groin.

The third one charged the Seal just as the first one grabbed the smaller man's ankle. All four of them were down, scrambling, and the whole place broke into a brawl.

George held his place at the bar, using his forearms to fend off anyone who moved in too close. Using his hands, feet or fists would only have resulted in another brawl. He was more interested in the initial scrimmage, and watched as the Seal rose from the fray and began kicking heads. Another sailor charged him from behind with a raised beer bottle.

George had seen enough. He grabbed the wrist of the bottle wielder and jerked the bottle from his hand. The smaller man in the fight whirled to meet the new threat, and took in the situation at a glance. The surprised sailor, with his wrist still held tight, turned toward George.

The Seal flattened his nose with the heel of his hand, and kicked the man's legs out from under him.

A loud roar erupted from the front of the bar as Shore Patrol poured in waving billy clubs.

The smaller man turned toward George, "You see my hat anywheres?"

George looked around and spotted a tan cowboy hat wedged between the legs of a barstool and the front bar kick panel. He grabbed it up and handed it over. He said, "C'mon, I've got a car out back."

More SP's at the back door waved them on through with barely a glance. George noticed the cowboy hat was back on the man's head. They got into George's car and the cowboy-hat-wearing Seal said. "It pays to wear civvies and stay sober around here."

George nodded and drove out of the alley. As they circled back past the front of the bar, he saw the SP's, teamed up by twos, tossing unconscious sailors into the back of a van, piling them right on top of each other.

"Holy shit!"

His passenger laughed. "They have to be meaner than the swabbies. My name's Steve."

"George."

"Where we headed, George?

I have a place not far from here. That eye is going to close up on you if we don't get some ice on it pretty soon. Your knuckles are skinned up too."

Steve looked down at his cowboy boots. "Got some shit on my boots too."

They kicked back and continued the conversation in George's apartment. "Where you from, Steve?"

"Cody, Wyoming."

"That's a long way from water."

"And that's why I joined the Navy. Ain't much else there either. How about you? This ain't your home either, I can tell."

They gave each other an abbreviated history. Steve Lewis was weathered-looking with washed-out blue eyes and thinning blond hair combed straight back. He was recently discharged after recuperating from surgery on his leg. "I was shot twice and knocked into the river. The first round hit something on my gear and knocked me over the side of the boat. I never found out what it hit because I was forced to strip it all off to keep from drowning.

"The second round hit my calf and lodged between the bones. The Portsmouth Sawbones wanted to take my leg off and I told them I would take theirs later. Anyway, I'm OK now—I just have to check in again in a month."

George didn't mention his first time in Vietnam, just the one where he was wounded. Then he asked, "What are you doing now, Steve? Working somewhere?"

"Nothing yet. I miss the action, but I didn't care much for Vietnam and I'm too old for rodeoing. I could do it though, but there ain't much money in it, and not much future. What about you?"

"I came down here to help out a friend. We're trying to recover some money for him, but we don't know where it's going to lead us yet. There might be some money for us in it too, but no guarantee."

They both sat back and thought about it for a couple minutes. George went and got another beer.

Steve said, "Recover, as in buried somewhere, or taking back from someone?"

George grinned. "Taking back from some real bad-asses."

"Sounds interesting."

"We'll probably be working around the edges of the law."

"Sounds like fun too."

"Steve, I like your style. Remember, I have a partner. Actually, it's his game. Let me get back to you."

Steve slept on George's couch that night and when they were leaving in the morning, they nearly collided with the upstairs neighbor. She was a cute little thing, maybe eighteen, with short, light-brown hair in a pixie cut, topping a shapely, petite body.

She gazed at Steve's black eye and gave them a radiant smile. "Hi Fellas. Rough night?"

George knew she was married to a sailor and that he was off at sea somewhere. He just laughed at the implication. He figured she was lonely but it was too close to home.

Steve grinned right back at her, "Not rough at all."

She addressed them both, "You know anything about plumbing?"

Steve bounced it right back at her. "Yours, mine or ours?"

She laughed a musical little laugh. "My toilet won't flush."

George stepped back and Steve said, "George was just taking me to get my tools. We'll be back in thirty minutes."

Once they drove off, George said, "Jesus, I was saving that for myself."

"No you wasn't or you would have already been at it."

"You know she's married, right!"

"To a sailor?"

"Yeah."

"OK."

An hour later, after Steve followed him back, George could hear them up there above his kitchen, grunting, squealing, thumping and shaking the walls. He knew from hearing it flush many times before that the bathroom was in another part of the apartment.

* * *

The following week, just after the Fourth of July, George received a letter from Murta with a Post Office box in Fredericksburg, Virginia as a return address. She told him she had secured a position as a night-shift manager at a major hotel. The position included lodging for her and Marisol.

She hoped George would be able to come and visit before long, and that Will would be able to finish his business soon.

George hadn't told Will, but he visited Murta and Marisol at the duplex a couple of times while Will was out scouting. He was looking forward to the time when he and Murta could be alone. He could tell she would like that too.

A couple days later, Will and George went out to Pap's to look at guns. George asked Pap about access to the barge and the property behind it.

"It belonged to my brother. He passed three years ago, and we just ain't done nothin' with it. When deer season comes, you can hunt back there with us. We've got several stands in good spots."

Although Pap knew what was going on, their business in the back room was with Lester. They wound up buying a Winchester Model 70 rifle with a mounted Redfield 3-9 scope, in .270 caliber, and three model 1911, .45 autos. They also picked up two Smith and Wesson model 36, .38 caliber revolvers, one with a two-inch barrel and the other with a three-inch barrel. This set them up with common-ammo autos and common-ammo revolvers. They also bought a Winchester Model 12, 12-gauge shotgun with a modified choke. George and Will were both familiar with this shotgun, billed as The Perfect Repeater. It held seven shells in the tube and one in the chamber. A man could fire it as fast as he could work the short-action slide.

Lester led them to a wooded area a few miles away to try out the guns. A rutted two-track through waist-high weeds led them past a burned-out shell of a house to an open area backed up by a hill about a hundred yards away. The shotgun was for multiple targets, close up or through walls. It worked fine, with no advantage to either of them.

It quickly became apparent George was superior with the rifle, but Will was better with the pistols. George wasn't sure how much better. It was close, but Will was close to him with the rifle too. One of the .45s wouldn't shoot accurately for either of them, and the slide rattled when Will shook it. Lester tried it too and had no better luck. He took it back to his truck and returned with a different one that shot just fine.

"I'll replace the barrel and peen the slide, and that other one will shoot like new again."

During the previous week, Will came up with some new leads in tracking down Bustamonte and Company. When they got back to Craddock, they parked in front of the A-side as always, but went straight through and out the back where they entered the B-side. Will had moved his belongings over there. George caught on right away, but wasn't sure about the necessity.

Will left lights on in the A-side but blacked out the windows in the B-side with heavy blankets. Maybe it would give him an edge if someone tracked him down. George didn't think it would be much of an edge, but he still hadn't seen Will in action.

CHAPTER 25

Will

I RETRIEVED THE WALLET TAKEN FROM BUSTAMONTE'S DRIVER. IT claimed he was Ricardo Schiffer, age thirty-four. The address was a Norfolk street address, one I wasn't familiar with. It didn't take long to find it on my city map, but it was a part of the city I hadn't visited, so I drove by it to scout it out.

I altered my appearance somewhat for my reconnaissance. A moustache shades and a cowboy hat did the job. I added the boots and jeans too, in case I had to walk.

The address paid off. It was a large, square, two-story house with several entrances at the edge of a business area. I was able to observe it from seventy-five yards away in a Mom and Pop restaurant. I took a chance being in there, but it wasn't the kind of place Bustamonte would visit.

I watched a couple of cars come and go, but they entered and left by way of a driveway leading to the rear of the house. I couldn't see the drivers, but I saw a couple of passengers who looked Hispanic.

The following day I was back in a different car wearing working man's clothes, including a cap. I parked and lingered in an even-closer bakery over coffee and doughnuts while I watched, occasionally looking at my wristwatch as if waiting for someone.

Late in the afternoon, when I was about ready to leave, I began to doubt the wisdom of my watching from so close. Adolfo walked out onto the front porch of the house with a coffee cup in his hand. He stood there for a good twenty minutes, sipping his coffee and looking around before going back inside.

This was a large gain and we needed to step up our program. Previously, I had made plans to go out of town with George the next day. We would have to get the ball rolling afterward.

* * *

George and I bought weapons and ammo from one of his friends out by the swamp, and while we were out there, we held a little shooting contest between the three of us. George was the best shot with the rifle and I was the poorest, but we were all close. I came out on top with the pistol.

Actually, I was a whole lot better with a handgun or rifle than either of them would have believed. I never fired a pistol until I entered the Army, but it came natural to me and I practiced as often as I could. If I practiced on a frequent basis, it was only a matter of looking close at what I wanted to hit. I could have been a top contender, but I didn't want to go that route. I also mingled with some Special Forces men who were as good, or nearly as good. No matter what your talent, or how good you are at it, somewhere out there is someone slightly better.

On the way back to Craddock, George told me about Alphonse and Steve Lewis. I agreed we needed the manpower, but pointed out we could only pay them day rate until it was over, with a possibility of nothing more. He was sure Alphonse would be good with it, and probably Steve too.

When we returned to Craddock, I moved the white Oldsmobile with the green top around behind the B-side of the duplex. We left the long guns in the trunk of it and each kept a set of keys.

Once inside the duplex, we opened a couple beers and I told him about finding the boarding house and Adolfo's presence there. "With Bustamonte's brother and his driver out of the picture, Adolfo has to be his bodyguard now, so he must be there too."

George said, "We don't know for sure where the money is yet, and what about the people he's taking? We need to find out where he holds them too."

"I know, and we do need more people to watch the warehouse area. I doubt they've had time to find an alternate place like that." We finished our beers and started a second round.

"George, I don't intend to take on Bustamonte's whole army. Once we find the people and the money, we'll move. We'll treat the organization like a snake—I intend to cut off the head whether or not I skin the rest."

"You mean kill Bustamonte."

"Yes, and Adolfo too. Can you do Bustamonte? I want Adolfo all to myself. He stuck a dagger in me."

"That's exactly what I had in mind when I picked out the Model 70. I would do it for free, just for what they did to Murta and Marisol—what they tried to do to you too." We shook hands in agreement. Afterward, George left for home.

The next day I met Alphonse and Steve at the Webster Avenue address, and liked both of them. Alphonse was older than the rest of us, but seemed willing to follow orders. He was as sharp as a tack too.

Steve had that rugged cowboy look. If you looked closely, you could see fine scars on his face from lots of fights, maybe not all from winning. Obviously, he hung in there either way.

Once we explained the situation and our tentative plan, Alphonse spoke up.

"I have something to bring to the party too, but it'll cost you."

I glanced at George. He seemed as surprised as I was. "Go ahead."

"I've got two Prick-10's and three Prick-6's, and extra batteries."

What a bonus. I could only say, "How much?" The PRC-10 Army FM field radio could be carried as a backpack, but was bulky and heavy. It had a great range of three to twelve miles though, and made a great base station for the hand-held PRC-6 Walkie-Talkies. The PRC-6 had a range of up to a mile. All five radios could be synchronized, or alternate frequencies could be used if you wanted one or more separate.

We agreed on a price and Alphonse said, "When it comes to slavers, I'm all for taking out the whole damn bunch."

Steve said, "I'll second that."

We laughed and I told them about my snake theory. They agreed with the idea. The two of them seemed to get along and they would be a real bonus for us.

I said we still needed more manpower, and Alphonse said a cousin who'd lost his arm was reliable, and the man needed money. "He can do more than you'd think and keep his mouth shut too. His name is Grady." Last names were never offered for Alphonse or Grady and I didn't make an issue of it.

So now there were five of us. The next day I visited War Howell at the Portsmouth Naval Hospital and told him the basics. He mentioned a trusted Marine friend named Sonny Metz who lost the tips of the middle and ring fingers of his left hand. He would muster out in a couple days. I told Warren to give him my number.

Grady was a sad-faced, hunched-over man about forty years old. He was bald on top, with thick hair on the sides. He looked half-asleep when we met him, but the impression was a fooler. He was quiet but alert and intelligent.

Sonny Metz, short and muscular without appearing stocky, was from Weston, West Virginia. He had curly, light-brown hair, intelligent blue eyes and an easy grin. I could tell he was a tough little monkey too. He said he would furnish his own firepower, another .45 auto, and his own handloads.

Now we had a team. The plan was forming.

CHAPTER 26

THERE WERE THREE TARGETS TO WATCH, THE HOUSE, THE YACHT AND the warehouse. It seemed logical that any staging of captives at the warehouse would be at night. Anything might transpire at the big house or the yacht at any time. Alphonse or Grady would be conspicuous close to the house, but either might get by as a dockhand looking for work near the yacht. Observing the warehouse at night, either of them would be nearly invisible if they were careful.

We needed a base within radio range midway between the three points so Alphonse found us an unfurnished apartment in a colored housing project. An extra hundred dollars a week guaranteed no one would bother us or our vehicles. Because the four of us white men would stand out, we decided to use a van to transport us in and out, rather than individual cars.

It would only be necessary to have one man there to relay messages, but we could nap there between watches. I mentioned this to Grady, and two cots, two chairs and a small table soon appeared. The following day a coffee pot with coffee and cups showed up too.

I called War's grandfather and asked if he knew where I could get a van. He owned one, a well-used, flat-nosed Chevy with a column shift. I had Sonny Metz go around and buy it outright from him. The Television Service logo on the sides of the van were faded just enough to fit in with the neighborhood, and established a purpose for it being there.

We got Alphonse and Grady to start watching the warehouse from just after dark until an hour before dawn. They quickly found a place on a rooftop where one could nap while the other watched. Sonny and Steve hit it off, joking occasionally about their differences in Service. They were both under the Navy umbrella though, and mutual respect was evident. They alternated watching the house.

Steve proved to be adept at altering appearances too, not just for him, but for others as well. He said, "It's all part of Seal Team training."

For the time being, we didn't watch the dock, reasoning that any actions at the warehouse or unusual activity at the house could prompt a move in that direction. Our best guess was Bustamonte alternated between the house and the yacht.

George and I discussed at length how we might take out Bustamonte and Adolfo. We came up with the idea of using a dump truck as a moving base to either shoot from, or to seek cover in after the shooting. A five-yard dump truck would have high-enough sides and the bed would be virtually bulletproof. Despite his missing arm, Grady had driven dump trucks in the recent past and knew where we could borrow one. He was certain it wouldn't be missed as the construction project had come to a halt over litigation.

Like Sonny Metz, Steve Lewis stated he would furnish his own weapons. We didn't find out what they would be until we assembled at the apartment in Norfolk. He brought in a faded tan duffel bag. Once inside, he pulled out an ArmaLite AR-15, the predecessor to the M16, and the first we'd seen. He assured us he had enough ammunition for more than one sustained battle. He also showed us two KA-BAR knives with seven-inch, clip point blades. We were all familiar with them and Sonny Metz also had one.

Next, he came up with a pair of 9mm, Browning High-Power, semi-automatic pistols. He displayed a brace of shoulder holsters and four, full, thirteen-round magazines to go along with them.

I surprised everyone by dumping out a bag of doeskin gloves in medium and large. They all picked out a pair and promised to use them from there on out. Grady only needed one, so there was an extra left-hand glove.

* * *

We watched for a week-and-a-half, well into August, with nothing happening. My money was running low. I didn't know what I'd do if I ran out. George had some, but I didn't think it was much, and I didn't want to take his anyway. The men were starting to get restless too. We moved them around to different posts to relieve the monotony. George and I took turns filling in for one or another so they had some personal time. I had to be careful about showing myself near the house or the yacht. Adolfo and I had been eyeball to eyeball.

Steve made us up different disguises from his bottomless duffel bag. George knew how to make up and use disguises too, which surprised me. I knew from the first time I met him that he worked on the edge—on the dark side. George was close to my age, but that still seemed young for what he'd been doing.

I got the impression that because he was bigger and I was smooth muscled, he thought he might have to become the deciding factor in a battle. Little did he know.

We needed to get to a dojo where we could test and enhance each other's skills. I kept up my own solitary routine to stay in shape and beat on inanimate objects to keep my hands, arms, feet and legs toughened up when no one was around. Trees were good for the feet, legs and edges of the hands. They were not good for fists or fingers though. A stuffed duffle bag worked better for that.

I knew George would be a rough customer, but didn't know the extent of his training or how he stayed in shape. I was sure he was underestimating my skill set. Throw Steve and Sonny into the mix and it could get real interesting. As old as Alphonse was, I didn't doubt he could still carry his weight too.

* * *

Then, finally, things started happening, and with a rush. George and I were both in the Norfolk apartment sleeping when the radio blipped static mixed with words before settling down. The clock read 3:30 a.m.

Alphonse's voice came through and he was breathing heavy. "A light-colored Chrysler showed up at the warehouse and a big sliding door opened. A minute later, a semi arrived and pulled up behind the car. Six dudes got out of the car with long guns. You there?"

George was getting dressed, so I answered. "Yes, go ahead Alphonse."

"The truck driver couldn't back up too good, so he only put the trailer partway into the warehouse. Four of the men with guns stood around on the outside, while the other two went inside. I couldn't see a whole lot, but I know they were unloading a bunch of people—lots of women and kids."

"What happened after that?"

"I left Grady there to watch and I got far enough away to call you."

"Good. Can one of you follow the car when it leaves?"

"I can, even though I'm driving that shitty Falcon. I don't think they'll be speeding."

"OK, great. I'll get everyone else ready to go."

George was in another room on our alternate frequency, talking to Sonny, who was near the house in the Studebaker. Steve was off somewhere else, sleeping, but he was on the same frequency as Sonny. We were ready but didn't yet know which way to go.

Alphonse said, "Moving." and clicked off. The radios went silent.

Two minutes went by before Grady's voice came through, just barely above a whisper. "The truck is leaving. What should I do?"

"Grady, this is Will. Can you follow it?"

"I got to get down off this roof, but I think I can catch up to them. That semi can't move too fast."

"Go! Call when you can."

Ten more minutes went by, then Alphonse came back on the radio. "I had to turn off, but they're heading for the big house."

"OK, park, but not too close."

"Roger that."

George appeared in the doorway holding the other radio in his hand. I nodded for him to speak, but I knew what he was going to say.

"A tan Chrysler New Yorker just pulled up to the house. One man went into the house through the front, but there's more people in the car. Sonny can't tell how many."

I quickly filled him in and let him know that Alphonse was standing by.

George's radio squawked again. I heard him say, "Follow it." Then he turned to me. "The man came back out of the house carrying a heavy suitcase. He took off in the car."

"Payoff money," I said.

George nodded and we headed for the van, grabbing Steve's duffel and our own weapons as he moved. He drove while I radioed Steve on George's radio. My PRC-10 was still tuned to Alphonse and Grady.

Another couple minutes of silence elapsed, and then Sonny's voice came through. "We're going through the tunnel to Portsmouth. I think I just passed Alphonse in the white Falcon."

"Stay on them."

Grady's voice came through on the other radio, so I picked that one up. "Will, they at a restaurant, eatin'. They left the truck in the alley."

"All right Grady. If you can, get the license number of both the tractor and the trailer. And a description of the truck and trailer too."

"No sweat, man. What you want me to do after that?"

"If you don't mind, go back and watch the warehouse. Don't get too close. It'll be daylight soon."

"All right, Will." Then he clicked off. Grady was the only one of us driving his own car, a faded, dark-blue 49 Plymouth coupe like one I'd owned in Florida.

Steve, farthest away, was driving George's black Ford.

* * *

When George and I arrived at Webster Avenue, we parked the van and stayed in it, waiting for Steve to show up in the Ford. It was a strange feeling with no one else on the streets or sidewalks. The morning was cool and still and the only sounds we heard were our own.

While we waited, George said, "When Steve gets here, let me and him take the Olds to catch up with them. It's the fastest."

"Good. I'll wait for Alphonse and follow up in your Ford."

We didn't have long to wait. The Ford rolled to a stop in the street and I motioned Steve to get out. George handed him his duffel and ran to the Oldsmobile, motioning Steve to go with him.

I jumped into the Ford and circled the block, waiting for Alphonse. He was there in another minute, but could only find a place to park a block farther on. I followed him and made another circuit while he parallel parked. He jumped in with me before I came to a full stop, so I kept driving and handed him the radio. Once we were out of town, Alphonse handed the radio back.

Steve and I talked on the walkie-talkies while George drove the Oldsmobile. We decided to alternate which cars were following closest, hoping the men we were after wouldn't spot us. I hadn't forgotten how I'd been made while tailing Adolfo. It was all different from my time in Army Intelligence in Europe, where I used shank's mare, taxis, buses and streetcars.

Sonny came over the radio and said, "Now they are headed down Highway 17, toward North Carolina."

Steve told him we weren't far behind, and to pull over somewhere so they could pick him up in the Olds. It was taking a chance our targets wouldn't turn off somewhere, but there were few places to turn off along that deserted highway.

We were closer than I thought. Sonny had pulled the Studebaker into the weeds alongside the road and was running toward the stopped Oldsmobile when Alphonse and I sailed past.

I put the hammer down and George stayed right behind me. In a couple minutes I saw the faint glow of taillights up ahead and let up on the gas. George dropped way back and let me ease on up on the car alone. It was the Chrysler.

We maintained a steady sixty-five as we passed the darkened Pap's truck stop, Alphonse and me in the Ford: George, Steve and Sonny in the Oldsmobile. We rolled on and I stayed a discrete two hundred yards behind the Chrysler. Three miles farther on, I saw headlights coming up fast behind me. I maintained my speed while Alphonse looked in the visor mirror and told me it was George. It was almost daylight and I knew this cat-and-mouse game couldn't go on much longer.

The Oldsmobile flew by doing at least ninety and stayed in the left lane. He never let up and I saw him pass the Chrysler the same way. We maintained our speed and the Olds went on, out of sight.

Another couple minutes went by and I knew we were getting close to the state line. There hadn't been anything on either side of us but brush and weeds for miles. The only feature other than the water-way on the right, was a ditch paralleling the road on the left.

The brake lights on the car in front of me flashed on. Like any early-morning driver, I didn't hit my brakes until I was close behind him, at least close enough to see what was going on. Beside me, Alphonse racked the slide on a .45 and slid it under my right thigh, safety on. He immediately grabbed another one and did the same, but held it down between his knees.

The brake lights in front of me went off and the Chrysler gained new life——but not for long. He swerved slightly to the left and I realized he was dodging the Olds stopped on the edge of the road. As we went by, I saw George rising from the weeds in front of it.

Fifty yards past it, Steve popped up from the ditch on the left and fired a burst from the AR-15, full auto, right into the driver's side windows of the Chrysler.

The car swerved wildly back and forth and veered off into the ditch on the left, where both the hood and the trunk lid popped open. I stopped just past the Olds.

George was out of the weeds and right beside me when I stopped, but then he ran on past. Sonny ran up to my right front fender from somewhere in the weeds, and stopped with his .45 in-hand, hanging down by his side.

Steve went around to the right side of the Chrysler as he ran up, never taking his eyes off the car. George ran up on the left side and peered inside, then fired one shot into the car.

Steve and George yanked all four of the doors open and three bodies spilled out. That left three still inside. George leaned into the front and fumbled around while Steve reached into the trunk and pulled out a big, cream-colored Samsonite suitcase.

Steve ran back to my Ford, opened the back door, and tossed the suitcase onto the floor behind my seat saying, "Let's roll." Then he ran back to the Olds, with George following.

Sonny jumped in with us and, as soon as he was clear, I backed up past the Olds and zigzagged back and forth, turning around. It didn't take them long either and we drove back to Portsmouth at a steady sixty, a hundred yards apart. I pulled over once to let Sonny take the Studebaker, and Steve and George passed me by in the Olds.

When we drove back within radio range, we heard Grady pleading with us to answer.

CHAPTER 27

GRADY WAS BACK TO WATCHING THE WAREHOUSE. I REGRETTED NOT leaving Alphonse in Norfolk with him. He was alone and there were five of us on this side of the river. I keyed him up.

"Those people are still in there, Will. I see light at the bottom of the big door."

"Grady, as soon as I can get to a phone booth, I'm going to call the police and tell them there are kidnapped people in there. Stick around until you see the cops show up, then go back and see if the truck is still at the restaurant."

"Oh, they still there. I let the air outta all three tires on one side of the tractor. But that ain't all!"

He paused for breath, "Will, I broke the padlock on the trailer door and looked inside. When I opened it up, the smell almost knocked me over. It was shit, man! Human shit——and piss all over the place inside there. And guess what? There was a dead kid in there too, up at the front." He stopped for a moment.

"What happened then, Grady?"

"I hung the broken padlock back on the trailer door, wiped down everything I touched, and got my black ass outta of there. When I was sure I was clear, I called the po-leese and told 'em about the truck and the drivers. I didn't give 'em my name."

"Outstanding, Grady. You're going to get a bonus for that. I'll have someone come and relieve you soon."

I got on the radio to fill George in on what Grady told me. He said he and Sonny were going back to the dock to watch the yacht.

Earlier, Steve scouted the top of an empty two-story building, a location where a shooter would have a good view of the yacht. We finally found out the name of the yacht was Abriana. Steve told us that in Portuguese it meant Mother of Many Nations.

The distance was about five hundred yards; close enough for a good shooter with a scope, but far enough away that he wouldn't be seen.

An alley ran behind the building and the dump truck could park there. A man could climb up on the truck cab and reach a pull-down fire escape.

When we reached Portsmouth, I stopped at the first phone booth I saw and called the State Police in Norfolk. An older man's raspy voice answered, "State Police. Is this an emergency?"

"I just saw six men herd at least fifty people from the back of a semi into a warehouse, prodding them with machine guns like sheep, most of them women and kids."

"What's your name, and where are you?"

I recited the address and door number of the warehouse, and then said, "You'd better hurry. They're probably abusing them already. There's little kids!"

Again, he wanted to know my name and location, and he sounded pissed off. I said, "Send all the cops you can get. NOW! GOD DAMN IT!" Then I hung up. I was pissed off too.

Afterward, I radioed Steve and asked him to watch the big house. Alphonse could join him after I drove him back to the Falcon. We drove to the duplex in Craddock and locked the suitcase in the B-side. Alphonse and I made a quick count of the money. There was a little over $26,000 in mixed bills: 20's, 50's and 100's.

I drove Alphonse back to Webster Avenue. On the way, I received another call on the radio from Grady. He said at least thirty cops showed up, surrounded the warehouse, and were forcing their way inside.

"People were coming out windows all around the building, man, some of them shooting. The cops were shooting too. I had to get out of there before I was caught up in it."

"Grady, you've done more than enough. Go on home and get some sleep.

"Oh, Grady, we did score some money too. You'll get at least a couple grand."

There was silence on the other end for a few seconds before I heard him say, "Man, man, man," followed by, "Over and out."

CHAPTER 28

George

GEORGE, STEVE AND SONNY RENDEZVOUSED AT THE SAFE HOUSE AND Steve took the Oldsmobile back to watch the big house. It was full daylight on a Sunday morning and there wasn't much traffic.

George drove Sonny to the dump truck, dropped his gear in the cab, and parked the Studebaker several blocks away. Sonny waited while he walked back then drove him to the alley Steve had shown them on the map. Once they were out of sight behind the building, George clambered from the cab up into the bed. Sonny reached up with his gear bag and George pulled it up with him.

He heard the radio squawking from inside the bag and pulled it free. It was Will.

"George, I just heard from Steve that there's a lot of activity at the big house. They must have gotten word about the raid. I'm almost there myself, but some of them might be heading your way."

"Roger that, we're in position, so I'm going on up." He double-clicked off and leaned out over the cab on the driver's side. "Sonny, things are happening. I'll give you two thumps on the cab roof when I'm ready to leave."

An arm reached out from the window and the hand patted the roof twice in acknowledgement. Sonny could snooze in the cab while George was on the roof. If anyone came along, he would just say he was hiding from his boss.

George could barely reach the edge of the roof from the railing on the fire escape. He didn't know how much of a parapet there was, so he took off his belt and looped the buckle end into the duffle bag strap. He gently lowered the bag over the edge using the belt, and felt it touch down about three feet below the edge just before he ran out of belt.

He let the belt drop and hoisted himself up and over. The height of the parapet was just right for him to crawl around on his hands and knees and remain undetected. When he reached the other side, he pulled out his binoculars and peered over the edge. Steve was right on the money. George had a clear view of the Abriana. The deck was about eight feet higher than the dock and a wide gangplank extended down to it. George could see the captain staring out over the piers from the wheelhouse.

In less than fifteen minutes, a black Cadillac drove out onto the dock and stopped just short of the gangplank. Two men stepped out of the car, Bustamonte and Adolfo. There was just enough time for George to get his Winchester ready before they arrived.

The two men moved to the rear of the car and opened the trunk lid. George moved the rifle into position and watched them through the scope. He wanted to shoot Bustamonte before he reached the gangplank so he could observe the body after it fell. If it moved, he would shoot again... but he knew that wouldn't happen. He was curious though and wanted to see what they were going to do.

They leaned over and hoisted a large, brown steamer trunk up to the edge, obtained a better grip, and sat it on the ground. Bustamonte straightened from his end and headed for the gangplank.

The wait was over. George timed Bustamonte's slight head movements as he walked and squeezed off his shot. A spray burst from the other side of Bustamonte's head less than ten feet from the ramp. His body fell in a heap at the foot of it and didn't move.

George quickly shifted his aim slightly while he chambered another round. Then, fearing the yacht would leave with captives aboard, he shot the Abriana's captain in the upper chest as he peered down at Bustamonte's body.

In his peripheral vision, George saw Adolfo moving at the back of the car and swung his rifle that way, but it was too late.

He heard tires squealing as he re-oriented his scope. The Cadillac was racing away and the trunk was gone. Somehow, Adolfo heaved it back into the car.

George stuffed his binoculars and rifle in the bag and scrambled across the roof on hands and knees. He slung the bag over his shoulder and lowered himself over the parapet. From there he dropped onto the fire escape eight feet below, and another nine feet straight down into the bed of the dump truck.

Sonny started the engine when he heard the shots. As soon as George slapped twice on the roof, the dump truck pulled away. Before they reached the end of the alley, George slung his duffle bag in through the open passenger window and followed it down, slithering in while Sonny was winding through the gears.

George continued down into a squat in the passenger footwell so he would be out of sight. As they drove away, he could smell the age in the truck from the exposed foam rubber and cracked plastic in the seat, and from the heat-activated engine and transmission grease near his face. When Sonny clutched and shifted, dust motes rose through a crack in the rubber boot around the stick shift coming up through the floor, causing George to sneeze. In less than two more minutes, they arrived at the Oldsmobile. During the ride, Sonny said, "You said only one shot."

George laughed, "Per man!"

"You shot two?"

"Bustamonte and the captain of the boat. Adolfo got away."

In a few minutes they were at the car. When Sonny stopped, George jumped down and pulled the bag with him. Sonny drove on and George threw the gear in the trunk of the Studebaker and drove smoothly away himself. Sonny would abandon the truck near where they stole it.

George started a roundabout route to make sure he was clear before picking Sonny back up. He stopped almost immediately though and retrieved the radio from the trunk, got rolling again, and keyed the mike. "Will, the sun is up."

"What about number two?" Will replied.

"I saved him for you, but I think he's hauling ass with the money. It's in a big, brown, wooden trunk with brass corners and latches. He's driving a new, black Cadillac, headed your way. I took out the captain though."

"Captain?"

"Of the Abriana."

Before Will could respond, Steve's voice came over the radio. "I have the Cadillac in sight."

George stayed silent while Will answered. "Stay after him but don't let him see you. Give us locations."

"On it! Locations coming up."

While the conversation was going on, George could hear sirens in the distance, heading for the docks.

While George was driving around, he thought about Will. He knew Will had been in some kind of spook operations in the Army, but didn't know how deep he had gotten into it. Will seemed tough enough, even though he didn't look the part, and he talked a good game too. So far in this operation though, Will hadn't fired a shot. No one had except for George and Steve.

CHAPTER 29

Will

STEVE RADIOED THAT THE CADILLAC WAS CRUISING AROUND DOWN-town Norfolk, moving with the traffic, "Probably checking for a tail. I almost lost him a couple of times, trying to stay out of sight."

I spotted the Cadillac and radioed back. "I see it. I'm picking him up now. Let's run streets parallel to him on both sides. We'll double team him."

Steve double-clicked. The game was on.

Adolfo finally circled back around to the east and drove out to Virginia Beach. It was more open out there and that made it harder to track him.

We were past Labor Day and almost all of the houses along the beach were deserted, the rich owners back to acquiring more money, while their families were back in school or other pursuits. Some of the houses out there were boarded up while others were under part-time reconstruction from the latest storms. Police presence was practically non-existent from the off-season reduction in force.

George radioed that he had picked Sonny back up and they were about ten minutes behind us. Having three cars to track with would make things easier. I didn't think Adolfo made the connection on any of them. On the way out, he cruised through a Giant grocery store parking lot and two monstrous automobile dealerships covering several acres each. I hadn't forgotten he was a pro.

The Cadillac headed straight out toward the beach where the roads were straight and open, forcing us to stop where the houses were still close together. Steve showed up in the Olds and parked a block away. He and I were watching Adolfo's progress through binoculars when George and Sonny showed up beside me. I told George to join me and motioned Sonny to drive on and circle around in the Studebaker. I radioed him and Steve that we needed to park at least a quarter-mile apart. George took over surveillance while they drove off. I still hadn't had a chance to talk to him about what happened down on Route 17.

* * *

We could only watch Adolfo's antics in the Cadillac from a distance. Our cars would show up like sore thumbs if we tried to take him out there in the open in broad daylight.

Adolfo drove straight down onto the beach and along the water's edge for a couple hundred yards, then turned back up toward the road where he became stuck in the sand. He pulled a short-handled shovel from the trunk of the car and proceeded to dig his way out, alternately digging and reversing to the edge of the water, where the sand was packed tighter.

Scattered, unfinished houses stood higher up, between him and us. Down near Adolfo, they were in a higher-income bracket and farther apart, but most were storm-damaged and boarded up. Low dunes rose above them. I was down to the beach with Nina not long before, so I had some idea of my surroundings. A road ran along the downhill side of the houses, but they had waterfront rights since it wasn't safe to build closer to the beach.

Finally, the Cadillac retraced its original path and headed back up to the road fronting the big houses. I figured he was stalling, biding his time to see if anyone else came along. He turned south along the beach side of the houses and turned in at the fourth one down. The car disappeared from our view and I assumed there was a garage under that side of it. We could see that a balcony or deck extended out from it on the beach side.

There was no more activity, so George and I discussed our options. Either, Adolfo owned the house, or he was a squatter. My guess was he owned it.

We would have to wait until after dark and it would be a long wait. Only one or two of us would need to watch, so George and Steve left to bring us some food and water. As he was leaving, George said, "Toilet paper too."

They brought back a bag full of hoagies, snack cakes, cokes and the toilet paper. While one man scanned with the binoculars, the rest of us ate and afterward took care of personal business.

I knew that the beachfront side of most of the houses was boarded up, but I didn't know if the backside was too. One of us would have to explore and Sonny volunteered for the job. "So far, all I've done is drive."

Steve commented, "It's not over yet. We're a team and you're pulling your weight."

I gave a thumbs-up. George was busy watching while Sonny left, skirting around behind the dunes and then crawling back up them to peer over the top, tough going in that loose sand. The sun was fading and the shadows were long in front of us before he returned.

"The windows in back are not boarded up, but I didn't see any light or activity either. From that side, there is only one level. There must be a walkout basement and a garage below it in the front."

That was the way I remembered the houses too, although some had three levels from the front. We discussed it for a while and came up with a plan.

On rare occasions, people walked the beach at night and some of them built campfires. We decided that after dark, Steve and Sonny would walk along the beach gathering driftwood, and build a campfire, but not directly in front of the house. The fire would be a distraction and give them a vantage point. They would sit on the side of the fire away from the beach. If Adolfo saw them from the house, the fire would blind him and he wouldn't be able to tell which way they were facing.

George and I would go up the dune behind the house. From there, George would watch with his rifle ready, and I would go in alone. I had a white handkerchief, and I would wave it when I came back out.

If Adolfo came out, George would shoot him.

If Adolfo left in the car, Steve or Sonny would shoot him.

CHAPTER 30

It was a tiring trek through the loose sand, as Sonny claimed. It was almost 11:00 o'clock when we reached the top above the house and stopped to rest. By then, there was enough light from the moon for me to make my way down. On the off chance someone would be at the back of the house, I slithered over the top and went down headfirst on my belly so I wouldn't show a profile.

When I reached the back, I found a small deck with two steps leading down to the sand. What anyone would want back there, I had no idea. A single door led in from the deck and a picture window stood four feet to the right of it and beyond the deck. A smaller window, higher up, and three feet to the left, looked out over the deck. My guess was that it was a bathroom. No light shone from either. The door was solid wood with no windows or peepholes.

I placed my ear up against the door and listened for voices. What I heard instead was salsa music from farther inside. That was good. I checked, and the door was locked.

I got out my tension bar and lock pick. There were two locks, one in the knob and one above it, undoubtedly a deadbolt. Going on the assumption the one in the knob would be looser, and would pick easier, I attacked it first. Most likely they were keyed alike, and knowing the feel of the pins would make the deadbolt easier. If I was lucky, the deadbolt wouldn't even be locked.

It was locked, but I still opened both of them in less than five minutes——another useful skill courtesy of Uncle Sam.

I put my lock tools away and drew the .45 from a belt holster behind my back. I let it hang down by my thigh with the safety off. Any time I carried, it was cocked-and-locked, ready for action. Now, it was safety off.

The door hinged inward, on the left, so I stood to the right and slowly eased it open a couple of inches while listening for alarm beeps or sirens, or any human or animal sounds or smells, especially dog. None of them were present but I did catch a faint whiff of something I couldn't immediately identify.

A dim light showed, and I heard nothing but the salsa music in the background. I shifted the .45 to my raised left hand and eased the door open a few inches more. Now I could see I was looking into a hallway that opened into another room to the right, about fifteen feet in. A closed door on my left would be the bathroom. Six feet in on the right was an open, arched doorway, with no light showing.

I opened the door enough to step in and past it, then pushed it shut with the knob twisted and my thumb extended as a buffer. It closed and latched without a sound and I shifted the gun back to my right hand. I kept it in front of me and close to my body so if I was attacked, it wouldn't be knocked from my grasp.

I was almost to the arched doorway when a man I had never seen before stepped through it and headed toward the front of the house. He was about my age and height, but slender, with black curly hair.

He never looked my way and there was no time to waste. I leveraged my wrist over his shoulder, cupped my left hand under his chin, and jammed the pistol barrel into his right ear.

I hissed into his other ear, "Make one sound and I'll scatter your brains."

I felt him trembling and he attempted to nod his head. I started to drag him backward, outside to where I could silence him, at least temporarily. I hated the thought that I might be in the wrong house.

I hadn't gained three feet when I heard a banshee wail behind me. A woman leaped onto my back, wrapped her legs around me, and began clawing at my eyes. The smell was coming from her, a perfume.

I shoved the man away from me with my gun hand, grabbed her hair with my left, and bent forward. The man in front of me fell to the floor screaming. Another man stepped into the hallway from the room in front. This one I had seen before, from the warehouse. I was facing the man with the tattoo, the crooked nose and eyes too close together. He held a revolver in his left hand.

I continued my move and heaved the woman on over my head and on top of the first man. She popped right back up between us and whirled to face me. The man with the tattoo didn't shoot. That was his mistake.

I had no compunctions about it myself. I shot them both, her in the heart. His eyes were just far enough apart for a .45 slug, and that's where I put it. I lowered my gun and shot the screaming ninny on the floor in the back of the head.

I still hadn't seen Adolfo and I couldn't hear a damned thing. The screaming and the .45 going off in the hallway temporarily deafened me.

CHAPTER 31

George

GEORGE THOUGHT, IT TOOK HIM LONG ENOUGH, AS HE FINALLY SAW a crack of light from the door below. He tired from holding the rifle in position while looking through the scope, so he had switched back to binoculars. Now, as Will eased through the door below, he brought the rifle back into position.

The door closed and there was nothing to do but watch—just like old times.

A few seconds later, he heard a long, banshee wail, followed by two quick shots, a pause, and then a third shot.

All three shots sounded like a .45, what Will was carrying. George didn't know what the Brazilians carried. The men he and Steve killed down on Route 17 were white and carried revolvers. From their drivers' licenses, they were from High Point, North Carolina.

He heard Steve open up with the AR-15 from the front of the house.

George thought: Oh shit, they got Will and Steve isn't letting them leave.

George was irritated at Will for going in alone and at himself for not being in the middle of things. He moved his eye back to the scope, then reached up and refocused it on the back of the house. Door or window, I'm not letting anyone leave that house alive.

CHAPTER 32

Will

I COULD BARELY HEAR THE AR-15 OUT FRONT, AND GUESSED ADOLFO was trying to leave.

Steve wouldn't let him.

I was on my hands and knees. With a quick peek past the bodies, I could see around the corner into the living room. The only cover would have been a sofa and two padded chairs. Neither were good enough. The stairs to the floor below had to be through the opening on the left. Adolfo would have to come up through there.

I busied myself piling the three bodies on top of each other as a makeshift fortification, and then stationed myself prone behind them. Meanwhile, I exchanged the partially used magazine for a full one. Two more full ones rested in my left jacket pocket, so I moved the half-full one to my left hip pocket.

The jacket was a navy-blue, corduroy sports coat, similar to the one I took from Bustamonte's driver, buttoned closed. An unzipped or unbuttoned jacket or coat hanging loose could be yanked down to a man's elbows from behind and the assailant could control the wearer with one hand.

I settled in with my ears still ringing, sound reaching my brain as if through a blanket. I heard Adolfo's voice from below.

"Mr. Real! I know you are up there. What have you done with my woman?"

He was trying to draw me out, to establish my location by my voice.

Two could play that game. I could use a little psychology of my own. I cupped my hand beside my mouth and turned my head so my voice would echo off the wall. "The puta is dead, and so is the man she was fucking!"

"Her brother? I don't think so!"

So, the ninny was her brother. "The pistolero!" I shouted.

He laughed before shouting. "No, he is a maricon too. He likes young boys!"

Maricon meant she-male and I knew better from the raping of Cynthia Leggit, where the man with the tattoo had cut off Cletus Arnold's hands.

It was time. The talking was about over and I readied myself. I had no doubt he was a slippery son of a bitch. He would be coming up on the left from the level below.

No sooner had I thought this than a pistol appeared from the corner, down at floor level. He fired randomly around the room without exposing himself. There were several shots from an automatic. It sounded like a nine-millimeter.

He was off the mark, and I shot the pistol, hoping to take the hand with it. The pistol went flying out of sight and I heard a yowl from around the corner.

There was several seconds of silence. I wasn't about to jump up and charge the doorway. My guess was, even if I crippled his hand, it would have been his left. He was probably ambidextrous. I recalled that when he braced me in the car he held the revolver in his right, but it might have been so I couldn't grab at it so easily. I hadn't forgotten how quickly he pulled the dagger from behind his neck and stuck it in mine——with his left hand. The revolver in his right hand remained steady while he did it. And, he probably still had the revolver.

"Mr. Real. You are a very good shot." His voice was stressed. Good.

"Hand-to-hand fighter too!" I replied.

"Hah, you want to fight me mano a mano? You are bigger than me."

"I don't think so, at least not enough to make a difference."

He thought about it for a minute. "How did you kill Gigante?" His voice was growing calmer and stronger.

While we were talking, I was crawling backward into the big room the ninny had come from. I was looking for anything I could use as a defense against him.

"Gigante was stupid!"

He laughed, "That is so, like a child. One who pulls wings from flies."

I spotted something I could use. It was a heavy wooden serving tray with a solid brass handle at each end.

I laughed as well. "Come on up, throw out your revolver and your dagger. I'll take you on."

"Ah, you haven't forgotten. And what will you give up, Mr. Real?"

"My .45. That's, all I have." I moved back out of the room and lay behind the bodies again.

"You are moving around up there. I believe you want to fight me. I have limited options, so that is what we will do. Your friends will most likely kill me anyway, so let me meet you with bare hands."

"OK, come on out. I'm ready!"

"I am throwing my revolver across the room into the front corner. The Luger is somewhere behind me and useless."

The big revolver slid across the front of the room and thudded against the wall on the far side.

"The dagger too!"

The dagger followed, skittering across the floor, and I heard the point stick in the baseboard. He was damn good with it.

"Now you, Mr. Real!"

"Show yourself and I will. I don't know what other weapons you have down there."

He popped his head out at waist height and drew it back, just long enough for him to see me behind the bodies with my pistol braced over them with a two-handed grip.

He knew I could have shot him, but didn't, so he stepped on up and out. His right hand was still behind the doorway.

"All the way out Adolfo!"

He took two sidesteps into the open with his hands raised palm-out at shoulder height. He was as dark and lean and deadly looking as a cobra.

"The gun, Mr. Real."

I slid the .45 across the floor toward the front corner and stood up. I kept my left hand behind my back, my right hanging at my side. My other Colt was nestled in the shoulder holster under my left arm.

He glanced over at his left hand, where blood was running down across his wrist and under his sleeve.

"I am going to lose my finger."

I had already noticed the pinky was dangling by a thread, so I didn't look again.

As quick as the snake that he was, his right hand dipped behind his neck and the dagger came at me like a bullet.

I whipped the tray up in front of me with my left hand and the dagger thudded into it with a solid thwack. The other tray handle whacked me on the bridge of the nose.

The dagger buried to the hilt and the point jutted through only an inch from my throat.

My right hand was on my chest, as if protecting my heart, as I stepped over the bodies. If he came up with another weapon, I would shoot him where he stood.

Instead, he let out a roar and charged me with a flurry of kicks and strikes.

It was karate—the real deal—but I had been through it before. I absorbed some of his blows, parried others, and struck back with front kicks, side kicks and punches. When he started timing them, I grabbed his shirt and flung him over the bodies of his own people with a judo throw.

He came back up over them with a snarl, his training momentarily forgotten in his rage, and tried to uppercut me in the groin.

I grabbed his hair and yanked his head down to meet my knee on its way up. It flattened his nose and blood flew everywhere. His body flew up into the air from the impact, with me still hanging onto his hair. I let go of it and he flopped over onto his back.

It should have finished him, but it didn't. He lay there for a few seconds, shaking his head back and forth, blood drops speckling the floor on both sides of his head.

I was contemplating going after his other dagger and finishing him off with it when he rolled over and scrambled after my forty-five.

I let him get halfway back around with it before I shot him in the right eye with my other pistol.

The forty-five fires an awesome round. His other eyeball popped right out of his head and hung by the cord. I sat down on the body of his dead woman to get my breath.

"Will, Will!" I heard Sonny shouting from below.

"Yeah, I'm alright!"

Sonny stuck part of his head around at floor level where Adolfo's pistol appeared earlier, then ducked back. I could hear him talking to someone else below.

A few seconds later, he reappeared with a forty-five in his hand. Steve followed, carrying the AR-15.

They looked all around at the four bodies and the blood, inhaling the smells of it, body waste and gunpowder, trying to figure out what happened. The floor was painted with blood. I was covered from the chest down with it from Adolfo's nose and from sprawling out behind the bloody bodies. It dripped down my nose from where the handle of the tray hit me. More blood matted the hair at both temples and my cheeks where the woman clawed me.

"Holy Hell! What happened here?" Sonny asked.

Steve started to go around the three bodies to get to the back door. I stopped him. "Don't stick you head out there. George will shoot it off."

The handkerchief in my hip pocket was still white, so we found a broom and stuck it in the bristles. I opened the door just a crack and waved our makeshift flag out through it.

While we waited for George, Sonny and Steve went back down to get the steamer trunk out of the Cadillac. They broke one latch and pried the corner open with a Ka-Bar just enough to see if it held money. It did, lots of it.

George came in and looked at everything, muttering to himself. Then he said, "Damn, damn, damn! You look like shit, Will. Did you kill them all?"

I just nodded.

"From the looks of you, it must have been one hell of a fight."

"Adolfo wanted to take me hand-to-hand. But then he threw the dagger."

"And?"

I held up the tray for him to see. "He charged me."

"So, you fought and then he went for the gun?"

"Yes!"

"I would have loved to see it. Is any of the blood on your clothes your own?

"No, just what's on my face. The woman jumped on my back and tried to claw my eyes out."

We went through the rest of the house and found some money and jewelry, but not much, although the jewelry items were expensive.

There were two large bedrooms on the other side, each with a private bath.

George said, "I think I underestimated you, Will."

I just shrugged. There was nothing to say to that. I picked up the tray and took it with me as a souvenir.

We went on down the stairs and found the Cadillac backed halfway out of the garage. The steamer trunk sat on the ground behind it and Steve was guarding it by sitting on it while Sonny went to get the Olds.

George played a flashlight around inside the car and said, "Sweet Jesus!"

I went around to the passenger side to have look. A dead woman lay folded over facedown on the passenger's seat. One of Steve's AR-15 bullets had passed through the seat and caught her in the spine just below the neck.

George reached in, grabbed her hair, and pulled her head up. She was identical to the woman I shot upstairs.

"Twins," he said,

"No, triplets," I responded,

"Triplets?"

"Yeah, the guy in the middle of the pile up there is one of them."

Steve walked up. "Maybe you and I could start a club, L K A: Lady Killers Anonymous."

Neither George nor I responded. It was a first for me, but I wasn't so sure about Steve. But people think and say strange things during and immediately after a battle.

Right after that, Sonny showed up with the big Oldsmobile. We loaded up the money trunk, piled in the car, and got the hell out of there. A couple minutes later, we were forced to pull off and hide the car in an unfinished garage until after the first wave of cops passed by. I changed clothes while we waited, and was thankful that I thought to bring something along. I used the back of my flannel shirt to wipe my face down as best I could. George snickered at me during the whole process.

We stayed with the Olds while Steve and Sonny sneaked off to get the other two cars. One was in a different garage and one was hidden behind a copse of trees. It was dicey, and took most of the rest of the night, but we eased the cars out of there without getting caught.

It had been another long, hard day and night and I had forgotten all about Alphonse, so I radioed him on the way back.

"Will! It's been so long I thought youse all dead. Thought I could keep the money I found."

"You mean from down by the swamp?"

"No, no, from the big house. Cops never did show up there, so I went on in—back door standin wide open."

"Oh yeah?"

"I fount fit-teen hunnit dollas and some dandy kicks and threads."

Sometimes he lapsed into the speech of a different persona. I said, "Knock off the soul-talk. You can keep the fifteen-hundred dollars, the shoes and the clothes. I wouldn't wear them downtown in Norfolk though. Some of those Brazilians might still be around."

"You didn't get rid of all of them?"

"No, too many. Like too big of a snake, we could only cut off the head and a few inches of neck. The rest are still out there thrashing around somewhere."

"You ain't been reading the newspapers, man. After that raid where they freed all those people, the Feds are on a witch-hunt for Brazilians. They tied it in with the yacht shootings too, and found more captives out there, some as young as three years old.

"Not only that, word is out on the radio that a motorcycle gang down in North Carolina is saying the Brazilians double-crossed them, killed three of their men down by the swamp on U.S. 17, and took their money back."

"I'll be damned. Still, we need to walk softly for a while and shouldn't be flashing gobs of money. You and Grady work out stories about an inheritance or something. Just be sure to spend it in little dabs. We'll get back to you with more money later."

"OK man, you da boss—a goot one doe."

He clicked off.

Now there were some new headaches to think about. George and I drove on out to Craddock and went through my ritual of entering on the A-side to reach the B-side from the back. We lugged the steamer trunk inside but didn't open it. We were too tired. There was only one bed, so George went back to the A-side.

The next morning, I finally had a chance to talk about the chase. "What happened down there on 17? What were you doing out of the car?"

George grinned. "Steve and I worked that out. When we were far enough ahead to stop, he ran ahead and hid in the ditch. I waited until they were too close to stop, then jumped out in front of them with my hands raised, palms out."

I muttered, "Crap."

"They hit their brakes for a moment before deciding to run me over. There was more than enough time."

"What if they just started shooting?"

"I thought they would, and if I'd seen a gun I would have been back down behind the big engine in the Olds."

"OK, OK, what happened when you ran up to the car?"

"The driver was still alive, trying to restart it, so I popped him. The rest of them were dead."

"Or, he might have shot you when you ran up. Hell, George you won't live long enough for me to kick your ass."

He just laughed. "None of them were facing my way, and I doubt the other part of your statement."

We discussed how soon we should move the trunk to a new location. Neither of us felt it would be safe where it was, or at Webster Avenue, and we still hadn't opened it.

We also needed to figure out how to disburse the money to the others, and the Howells, so none of them would go on a crazy spending spree and draw attention to us all.

We had promised each of them a day rate plus ten percent after expenses. We promised Steve and Sonny more because they would be active players. Sonny hadn't fired a shot, but he was in the thick of it, regardless.

CHAPTER 33

THE PHONE RANG IN THE OTHER SIDE OF THE DUPLEX, SO I WENT OVER and answered it. The call was from Steve and he wanted to know if everybody else made it out OK. I told him we had, and that I would call him back when we could set up a meeting. He said he was in touch with Sonny and would let him know when and where it was.

I told him we hadn't even looked at the money yet. I knew that was what he was getting at.

He hung up and I went back to talk with George. Where in the hell could we hide the money?

We bounced it back and forth for a while and George said, "I have an idea. We already have a hidden car, the fifty-four Chevy. Let's hide the money out there."

"In the car?"

"No, that probably wouldn't be a good idea. I meant in Dismal Swamp itself."

"Bury it like pirates' treasure? That's kind of far-fetched, isn't it."

"Yeah, you're right."

We decided to go ahead and open the trunk and count the money. Sonny or Steve had broken one of the locking latches, but I just picked the other one. It only took a few seconds.

The trunk was about the same size as an Army footlocker, but deeper. The bills inside were laying loose, about two-thirds the depth of the trunk. It was a mess. Mixed, twenties, fifties and hundreds lay in a mound as if the Brazilians just threw them in as they passed by.

I stirred my hand around in them and received two more surprises. A layer of jewelry rested below the bills. I felt watches, rings, bracelets, necklaces, and something else. I pulled an object out to verify what I thought it might be. It was a human tooth with a big gold filling. I felt around again and brought up several, plus a couple of complete solid-gold teeth.

George helped me dump the whole mess out on the bed. Some of the bills fell off but we picked them back up. What I was looking for was a false bottom, and I found it. Underneath were several passports, duplicates in different names for the same people. Bustamonte, Adolfo, the three others I killed in the house, and even two for Gigante. There were also stock certificates, property deeds, mineral rights and bearer bonds issued by major corporations. Of these, only the bearer bonds would be worth the risk to cash in on.

"What the hell are we going to do with all this jewelry and gold teeth?" George asked.

"Well, there's no way of tracking it or getting it back to its original owners. It won't be traceable either. Those people never made it back."

"Let's just hold it back and not tell the others. It would be too much nuisance to try to evaluate it. We can keep it in reserve or move it back into circulation a little bit at a time as we travel."

That was copasetic and we shook on it. George scooped it up into two piles, one for each of us. He did the same with the bearer bonds. Finished with that, he moved all the other documents to a separate pile, and said, "What are we going to do with these?"

"Let's wait a while and leave them in a church, one we're sure will contact the police. Maybe some of the rightful owners will get them."

George agreed and we loaded it all into pillowcases, using them all up. We'd just have to buy more pillowcases. The ones with jewelry weighed out to between twelve to fifteen pounds each. We stashed half of all the loot in each side of the duplex.

Counting the money took longer. The total was $722,640.

"They must have been doing this for years." George commented.

* * *

We agreed to shift $75,000 back to the Howells. That would get them back on their feet. After expenses, the other four men would get varying amounts of over $62,000 each. Ultimately, George and I would wind up with over $180,000 each, plus what we could eventually get out of the bonds and jewelry. We still had to hide the bulk of the money before we invited any of the others out to the duplex.

George went into Portsmouth the next morning to look for something else to put the money in. While he was gone, I hid a loaded pillowcase up in the attic crawlspace on each side of the duplex. I didn't want to short the men, but we were fixing every one of them up with more money than they ever dreamed of. I was still worried one or more of them would go on a spending binge and expose us all.

I called my smart, tough and educated friend Robert Cee up in New York and explained the money situation to him without mentioning the bonds and jewelry. He promised to do some checking and call me back that evening with some creative ways for all of us to hide our money.

George came back with three rectangular beverage coolers, two metal Colemans and a plastic Igloo. The Igloo was smaller, so we put the money for our partners in that one. Money for the Howells and my share went in one of the Colemans, and George took the other. We stashed them in the attics too.

Next, I called Mr. Howell and asked him about the TV shops. He told me the mortgage company who held the lien sold the one in Norfolk. A local bank still owned the one in Portsmouth and it was listed through a local real estate agency. The listing was for just under forty thousand. If they sold it for that, he would still owe the bank fifteen thousand. He assured me it was intact, with merchandise still inside, but locked up.

* * *

The next day, a Sunday, we met the rest of the crew at George's Webster Avenue apartment for a business meeting. Alphonse and Grady brought the Chevy van we left near the apartment in Norfolk.

I addressed them all, "Fellows we should have had this meeting beforehand but we never anticipated collecting this much money. The main issue is that if any one of us draws attention to himself by spending extravagantly, we all go down."

There were murmurs and glances at each other, but no comments, so I continued. "I have a plan in the works where you could each reap the benefits of over sixty-thousand dollars without appearing to."

"How you going to do that?" Grady asked.

"Grady, you live in a multiple-unit apartment building and you are doing odd jobs for a living. Could you perform the duties of maintenance man for that building?"

"Shore I could, but they won't hire me. The man who has the job is a fool, but he's related to the owner."

"You could own the building anonymously and have the job. You could collect all the rents and invest them in a legitimate program while still keeping a good salary for yourself. You will never have to worry about money again."

Grady sat back in surprise, contemplating my suggestion.

I looked at Alphonse. "I know you've done some boxing and some backyard coaching, trying to keep kids out of trouble. How would you like to own a boxing-wrestling gym——and train both colored and white kids?"

He picked up on it right away. "I'd be the manager and head coach, and keep all the fees, right?"

"Yes, and you could rent out part of the building for extra income. You and Grady would have to act as collectors for the bogus companies that own the buildings.

"Or, even better, you and Grady could have papers showing you are owners with a mortgage on the properties. You would get a receipt for payments made every month, even though you won't be making any."

He looked over at Grady who asked, "How we going to get some real pleasure out of this money while we're waiting for things like this to happen?"

"Go to another state for a while, maybe visit with a fictitious old friend. While you're gone, spend a little money, but not excessively. Rent a Cadillac. Eat in restaurants. Just don't bring anything back home with you, not even new clothes.

Alphonse spoke up. "I can do that. I've got an old aunt in Mississippi. She'll be glad to see me, but she won't see much of me and she won't remember much after I'm gone."

"Not until after you've found the building you want." I answered. "Meanwhile you are working for an out-of-state property investment company, founded by an old Army friend."

There were nods all around and I saw George grinning. Steve spoke up. "I don't intend to stick around here. I want to buy some property down in Florida and maybe start a charter fishing business in the Clearwater area."

I gave him a thumbs up, and Sonny raised his hand. "I want to buy some property in West Virginia, maybe open a hunting lodge and a shooting range."

Grady said, "You goin' to let colored folks hunt an shoot there?"

Sonny answered, "Hell yes! You'll be the first one. Free admission."

"First man or first colored?"

We all laughed and the question went unanswered. I felt the tension in the room drain away.

"What about you and George?" Steve asked.

I looked over at George, because we hadn't discussed that, or even if we were going to stay in the area.

He said, "I'm just going to let mine sit and grow while I go back to school. My disability pension doesn't run out for a long time, if ever."

"Same here," I answered. Then I summarized the details. "Just as in any business, we aren't all getting exactly the same amounts, depending on what you did and the risks you took. If everyone agrees, I would like to be your investment manager. You've already got some cash and I have an envelope for each of you with five-hundred dollars and a slip stating what your investment amounts would be."

George passed out the envelopes and we watched as they opened them. There were smiles all-around and no dissent.

Steve spoke up first, which was good since the others looked up to him for his role in taking out the car down on Highway 17. "I agree. Can I pick out my own property and boat?"

"You'd have to." George responded.

The rest followed suit and we all shook hands. George produced a bottle of champagne and some water glasses and we all toasted our friendship and good fortune.

The next morning, Robert Cee called me and said he had set up a dummy offshore property investment corporation that could double as a mortgage lender. I could start buying property with cash as a corporate representative. We were on our way.

CHAPTER 34

George

GEORGE THOUGHT AT LEAST ONE OF THE MEN WOULD OBJECT AND demand all of his money on the spot. But then Grady had said, "I wouldn't even know what to do with even a tenth of all that money."

He was glad they hadn't demanded it and even more glad that Steve and Sonny wished to move to different states. They were the wild cards. He was sure they would be back if Will didn't follow through. He felt they would more than likely want to control their own fortunes. He certainly did.

George needed a place of his own but was in a conundrum. He liked the Webster Avenue apartment but everyone knew where it was, and the rental agreement was still in Will's name. He didn't feel that either side of the Craddock duplexes was safe either and decided that after everyone else left, he would just come right out and talk to Will about it.

When Will was getting ready to leave, he brought it up. "Will, I don't like the idea of having all of our money stashed in one place. If you leave to go anywhere, no one is guarding it."

"I've been thinking about it too. We each need a place of our own separate from our business interests. We have several loose ends to tie up."

"Such as?"

"The apartment in Norfolk, the van around the corner from Webster Avenue, the extra cars and the one you have stashed out in the swamp."

"You forgot to mention the buying up of all those properties."

"I'll take care of all that if you'll take care of the cars and getting clear of the apartment in Norfolk. As soon as you find a place for it, you can take your share of the money too. It's safer for both of us if we're split up."

"You forgot to mention one other thing, Will."

"Oh yeah, what is it?"

"The women. You've talked about Nina, but I've never seen her. As soon as I can get clear, I'm going up to Fredericksburg to see Murta."

"Good idea. She needs to know Bustamonte is gone and out of business. Why don't you look for a place up there? It's far enough away, but not too far if I need you."

They agreed and decided George should make a temporary move out to the B-side in Craddock while Will would go back to the A-side. That way, they could alternate taking care of business and guarding the duplex.

Within three days, Will purchased the TV shop for Mr. Howell and the apartment house for Grady. He promised Grady that when he returned from vacation Will would fire the maintenance man so Grady could take over.

Will told George that Howell didn't want the TV shop in his name again and would be happy as manager. Will's friend set up a trust fund for Howell. It would pay the utilities and give him a generous manager's salary for life. Howell wouldn't accept any other money, but he agreed to let Will store another safe in the storage room at the back of the shop. He also agreed to let them give the van back to him, gratis.

George enlisted Alphonse and Grady's help in getting clear of the apartment in Norfolk and two of the cars. Even though it had a damaged rear end, he liked the Oldsmobile better than he did the Ford, so he decided to let the Ford go. When he mentioned it, Alphonse bought it for himself. The Falcon didn't have much value, so George let Grady have it for a relative who needed a car.

After the business in Norfolk and Portsmouth, George went out to visit Pappy and his son Lester. When he mentioned getting the 54 Chevy out of the swamp so he could sell it, they wanted to buy it and leave it on the other side of the canal. It would save them walking around to keep track of their property and would be useful during hunting season.

Lester said, "That old bitch is as good as a Jeep back in there. It has high enough ground clearance and the green top makes it hard to see."

They bought the car and Old Bitch stuck as a name for it.

On the first day that Will was off taking care of business, George called Murta and told her the threat to her and Marisol was gone. She was excited to hear from him and told him she read about the shooting of Bustamonte and the freeing of captives from both the warehouse and the yacht. No mention was made of George or Will and she was concerned about both of them.

"Murta, we are both fine and I'm looking forward to seeing you soon."

"Please come quickly. I will reserve a special room for you in the hotel."

"We have a few more days of business to take care of before I can come and see you. I will call first."

"Is this business with Bustamonte's army?"

"No, they are all gone."

"Adolfo too?"

"He is dead, Gigante too."

"Did you kill them?"

"No, someone else did."

"I would not be unhappy if you shot him. He was an evil man."

George promised again to come and see her soon.

On his third free day, he drove out to Suffolk and looked at some rentals there. With no real ties anywhere else, he was thinking about staying in that area. Dismal Swamp called to him and he knew he could go in from the west side, south of Suffolk, without crossing the canal. A listing for a small three-bedroom house on the outskirts of Suffolk caught his eye, so he drove out to look it over.

The house had a full, walkout basement with a rear entrance. A wide back porch looked down over a wooded hillside and doubled as a carport. With some tough negotiating and a show of money, he managed to rent with an option to buy.

He bought an old Cary safe from a local locksmith as soon as he moved in. After the locksmith crew delivered it, he rolled it into the smallest bedroom in back and bolted it to studs in the wall with lag bolts. The locksmith showed him how to change the combination by removing the inner door panel and relocating the setscrew-pins. The next day, while Will was gone, he brought his money down from the attic and locked it in the trunk of his Oldsmobile.

The following day he told Will about the move. Afterward, he transferred his money to Suffolk. Will had already told him about moving his own money to the TV shop. George's money was now secure too.

During the tracking of Adolfo through the automobile dealerships, George spotted a big sign in a showroom window.

Experienced Mechanic Wanted.

He entered the dealership and looked at new, 1964 Fords for only a couple of minutes before a salesman approached and sent him to the Service Department in the adjacent building. The complex was huge, covering several acres, and when he reported there, a man directed him to yet another building. The process was repeated and he walked from building to building as directed, anticipating an interview.

It was a hot, humid, September day, and heat waves shimmered up from the asphalt of the parking lots as he walked from one lot to another. He could feel the softened pavement give under his steps as he walked. The heat rose up through his shoes and he could feel it burning the soles of his feet. At the fourth building, a man sent him back to the original Service Department.

The grizzled attendant with the graying flattop haircut said, "I told you to go to Building Nine."

"Yeah, well they told me to go to Building Seven. And I got more of the same, again and again, until I was sent back here."

The bigger, older man in his forties thought he could intimidate George. He leaned over the counter with both hands braced on the countertop, and growled right in George's face. "Well go back again, Dimwit."

George grabbed the man's collar, head-butted him in the nose, and gave him a shove. The man flew backward with blood gushing down the front of his shirt, and crashed into a display board with various auto parts behind him. He dropped to the floor in a sitting position and the items rained down onto his head and shoulders.

George turned on his heel and marched out. He expected someone to follow him, and he was looking forward to a fight, but no one came. He passed a man with the dealer's logo on his shirt just outside in the parking lot, but the man winked at him and gave him a thumbs-up. "That asshole's had it coming for a long time."

On his way back through downtown, traffic slowed to a crawl. He was looking around for a place to cool off and drink a beer when he saw something that made him do a double take. A bronzed giant was plodding down the street hunched over with his massive arms swinging from front to side as he moved along.

Two other men in their thirties with Brazilian features followed him at a respectful distance their heads turning slightly as they seemed to scan for unseen enemies. George drove on past without looking directly at them. He noticed the giant had an eye patch over his left eye.

He was anxious to visit Murta, but here was other business to take care of first. He needed to find out where the Brazilians were going and he needed to call Will. His thoughts of cooling off with a cold beer vanished.

He drove ahead for three blocks, parked and slumped down on the passenger side with a hat pulled down to shade his face. After they marched past, he stayed put until he saw them turn two blocks ahead.

The next time he parked on a perpendicular street so they would only pass behind his car from half-a-block away.

Afterward, he left the car and followed them on foot for a ways, mentally cursing that he was again walking in the heat of the day. Finally, he saw them enter an apartment building and noted the address and building number.

George returned to the car and moved it to where he could observe the building entrance. When no one seemingly related came or went for an hour, he left to call Will.

* * *

"Will, you will never guess who I saw in Norfolk just an hour ago."

"Murta?"

"No, she's in Fredericksburg. It's someone who would like to embrace you."

"Cut the crap George. Just tell me."

"Well Jack, falling from the beanstalk didn't kill the giant. He's walking around as big as you please."

* * *

After placing the call to Will, George drove back through the tunnel to Portsmouth. He had an address for an experienced mechanic. The ad stated, Apply in Person. It was a smaller ad and he assumed it wouldn't be as much of an opportunity.

The address turned out to be a surprise. It was a Harley Davidson motorcycle business in a good-sized building. George didn't know anything about motorcycles, so he sat in the car for a couple minutes, thinking it over.

Inside, at least twenty motorcycles of different sizes stood at different angles to display their best features. He noticed a few different brands, a couple he'd never heard of: Gilera and Ducati.

There wasn't a salesman in sight, so George looked them over. A man in a corner office gave him a slight wave through a large window, but left him alone to look. He was impressed with the overall appearance of both the motorcycles and the showroom. He squatted down to take a closer look at the engines on two side-by-side Harley Davidsons, one larger and one smaller.

"Find something interesting?" The man from the office was standing a few feet away with a friendly smile. He was thin, about five-foot-ten, with gray hair and glasses.

George said, "I see they are the same brand but they are built differently and the engine layouts aren't even close to the same."

"Are you a rider?"

"No, I'm a mechanic, but I don't know anything about motorcycles."

"But you seem to know something about engines and design. Are you here about the ad?"

"Yes, but it didn't say motorcycle mechanic."

The man stuck out his hand. "I'm Thomas Wheeling. This is my shop and you're right. There aren't many motorcycle mechanics around. You probably wouldn't have come around if it said that."

They appraised each other for a few seconds. George said, "I guess not. My name is George Rickson."

"Come on back to my office and I'll buy you a coke. It's cooler in there. I have air conditioning."

They sat down inside and Thomas told him some things about motorcycles, but he was more interested in hearing about George. George fudged some on his military experience working on Jeeps and trucks. He was surprised to hear Thomas was an Army veteran too and had been in Germany ten years before George.

Thomas finally said, "Why don't you come back in the morning and I'll let you work on one for a while. If you do all right, we can discuss wages. If not, I'll pay you for your time and try to convince you to become a rider."

George said, "I'm sorry but I already have other commitments tomorrow. I can't do it until Tuesday of next week."

"OK, I know I caught you by surprise. I'll see you Tuesday." They stood and shook on it. George left feeling good about the interview.

CHAPTER 35

Will

I wasn't too surprised when George called me on a Friday evening, but I was surprised about why. Gigantesco still alive and walking around——it was hard to believe. I couldn't let that go. We needed to put that sadistic killer down permanently. He had to be stopped no matter what his mental capacity. Since there were more of the Brazilians, there were probably more victims in captivity too.

George told me he planned to start a regular job within the next week or two, which surprised me, but that he would buy some time before starting on a full-time basis. He only saw two other Brazilians besides Gigante, so I figured the two of us could handle it. We agreed to meet the next afternoon.

George picked me up at Webster Avenue in his Oldsmobile and we drove on over to Norfolk to the apartment house. It was in a low-income area, the kind where people tend to mind their own business, so we parked, waited and watched. He told me about the potential job in the motorcycle shop. I had never ridden a motorcycle myself, but the idea appealed to me. I said I would stop by and look at them if he took the job.

Less than fifteen minutes after we parked, Gigante walked out of the building followed by two Brazilians. They went to a Chrysler parked about seventy-five yards away and drove off. Ji struggled his way into the front passenger seat after pushing it all the way back. The car squatted as he slumped down into it, and the door hung up on the sidewalk until the other two sat on the driver's side, one in front-one in back, to balance the car. There wouldn't have been any legroom behind his custom, bucket seat anyway.

We pulled out and followed them at a two-block distance. Less than half-a-mile later George said, "Someone is following us."

I pulled down the sun visor and looked in its mirror but I couldn't spot who he was talking about. "More Brazilians?"

"No, I don't think so, but I can't see them well enough to tell. It's a two-tone, white over blue, 62 Buick Hardtop with two men in the front seat. I don't think there's anyone in the back seat."

The parade continued, spanning four-to-six blocks, headed south toward Chesapeake. I didn't want to look conspicuous to the car following us, so I relied on George to keep me posted. I carried my forty-five in a shoulder holster over my T-shirt, but under a loose, partially-buttoned, long-sleeved shirt. I also had a lead-weighted sap in my left hip pocket. I was sure George was carrying, but I didn't know what weapons, or how many. The cars spread out on the open highway and George commented, "Still following."

We soon came to a forested area and the Chrysler turned in at a park entrance ahead of us. We drove on past for half a mile and the Buick followed us.

"Now we'll get a look at them," George said as he slowed, rolled onto the shoulder, and made a quick U-turn. As we headed back, he leaned forward and slid a .45 from behind his back. I didn't even have to ask if it was cocked.

He placed it under his right thigh and said, "Get ready."

I didn't bother to answer. Mine was already out and resting in my hand, pointed down between my feet. George ratcheted the seat back a couple of notches and leaned back farther. That gave me a wider field of fire through his window if it became necessary. Mine was already notched back.

We passed the newer Buick, both cars doing about forty-five. Two rugged-looking white men in their mid-to-late thirties stared at both of us as we stared back at both of them. "Looked like tough noncoms," George commented.

"Yep, not Brazilians. It must be me, George. I do have enemies. I just didn't expect any of them to show up here."

"Do you know them?"

"No, but that doesn't mean anything. They could be friends of enemies, or even mercenaries."

The park entrance showed up on our left and George turned in. As he did, he glanced back to the south, the way we'd come from, and said, "The Buick is coming back. You look ahead for the Chrysler and I'll keep an eye on the ones behind us. I don't think they have any idea we are following another car."

The dirt roads through the park were barely two cars wide through patches of woods and swamp. The Chrysler was stopped a quarter-mile in. Off to their right, a family with three small children sat at a picnic table with playground equipment in the background. A brown Plymouth 4-door sedan sat off to the side.

I said, "Oh shit!" because I realized what was going on. Families like this were easy pickings for kidnappers.

The driver of the Chrysler must have spotted us because he shifted into gear and moved on deeper into the park. My elbow was out the window and my pistol rested on the windowsill. I noticed George had his in his left hand, in the same position. The ability to shoot with either hand was a necessity for what we were doing. All three cars passed the picnic area and I breathed a sigh of relief. The family didn't know how close they'd come.

A hundred yards on, the Chrysler stopped, and then George suddenly hollered, "Bail out!" Our car rolled on for a few yards and stopped.

CHAPTER 36

I WAS BARELY CLEAR OF THE DOORWAY WHEN GLASS FLEW EVERY-where, instantly followed by the clatter of automatic rifle fire in bursts. I recognized the staccato bark of an AK-47 even as I hollered at George, "Oblique front!"

I saw him scrambling away through the brush hunched over, moving ahead. He knew what I meant. I wanted to direct the fire toward the Brazilians. I hoped the family we passed had enough sense to get the hell out of there. Along the way, I mentally cursed myself for not bringing the Model 12. In the brush, you didn't have to see exactly where someone was located to hit them with the shotgun.

As I zigzagged forward through the trees, trying to stay under cover myself, I saw the Brazilians flitting through the trees ahead of me. One of them turned and fired back toward me. I hit the dirt while a short burst from an AK-47 behind my position put him down. Another of the Brazilians started shooting from behind a tree and I stayed down, caught in the middle.

Ahead, and across the two-lane road, I saw one of the shooters move up past our car. He had an AK-47 too. They were both riflemen. When his partner started shooting again, the one across the road spun around and collapsed. From the return fire, they mistook the Brazilians for us, and George nailed him.

I eased backward, down into the swampy water behind the knees of a bald cypress tree, not concerned about snakes. All wildlife seems to know what gunfire is and disappear from the immediate area when they hear it.

The shooter on my side worked his way on past me and I let him go. Another pistol fired ahead of me and I saw Ji's big head poking around from behind a tree. The rifleman saw it too and hosed down that half of the tree trunk. I was sure the rifleman hit him. Apparently he thought so too as he kept advancing.

The other Brazilian stayed out of sight and the rifleman became far more wary. I thought about shooting him in the back, but I wanted him to get the Brazilian first, so I waited.

There was a crash in the woods ahead of me, followed by two pistol shots. They sounded like nine-millimeter, so I knew it wasn't George.

That was all the rifleman needed. The Brazilian exposed himself slightly when he fired and it got him killed. He was a good shot though, because he hit his opponent before collapsing.

I could still see the rifleman when he fell, but he popped right back up and slowly moved forward. He kept the AK-47 stock nestled into his shoulder and his head down behind the barrel as he advanced.

Finally, he stood over the dead Brazilian. He looked around and hollered, "Milton?" His partner didn't answer.

He continued anyway, "Who the fuck are these guys?"

I rose in the knee-deep water behind the tree and braced myself against the trunk. "Hey!"

He was good too. His AK-47 was more than halfway into its swing my way when my bullet hit him in the throat and snapped his neck. Afterward, I wished I had shot him in the arm so I could have kept him alive. I would have found out who hired them. I had a good idea though. They probably worked for ex-Colonel Boris Rathke, head of a group of weapons thieves and black-marketers I took down while stationed in France. Rathke was still doing time in Leavenworth, but he had friends on the outside and he vowed to get me. It was ironic that people were trying to kill me for things I had done legally, while no one was after me for those I killed outside the law. But then I thought of US Marshal Jerry Smith and his insinuation that smugglers, or Hiram Walker's relatives, may be after me. But after this long, I doubted that.

I eased on around through the trees checking on the Brazilians to make sure they were all dead.

They were.

A third of Gigantesco's huge head was mush from the AK-47 rounds, including his right eye. The patch was gone from the other one, the one I claimed. It was glazed over and milky white. He would be a blind man in Hell.

I felt a non-threatening presence beside me and George said, "We'd better get the hell out of here."

The Olds started right back up and we let it run while we knocked out the rest of the glass in the windshield and rear window with the AK-47 barrels. A single bullet had punctured the trunk, passed through both seat backs, and taken out the radio. The rest of the car was untouched. As an afterthought, we shot out the windows in the Chrysler with one of the AKs. We wiped down the rifles and left them behind, nestled in the hands of their owners.

The family with the brown Plymouth was long gone and we left without seeing any cops or hearing any sirens. To be on the safe side, we drove on down into North Carolina and parked out of sight until after dark. Our reasoning was that the missing windshield and rear window wouldn't be as noticeable at night.

While we waited, George told me his side of things. After we were back in there a ways, he saw a rifle barrel poke out the window on the passenger side. At the same time, the driver stuck a handgun out the window on his side. That's when he hollered, "Bail out!" He heard and understood me when I hollered, "Oblique front."

Both of the riflemen were wearing bulletproof vests. I suspected they were from the way the one I shot popped right back up when the Brazilian shot him.

"I never thought of a vest," George said. "I waited to time my shot so his partner wouldn't hear it, and shot him in the head so he wouldn't holler out."

We both agreed it started out bad, but wound up like shooting fish in a barrel.

I drove us back by cutting over to U.S. 17 and back up to Portsmouth, where we retrieved my Studebaker. Then I followed George back to Suffolk where he would stash the Oldsmobile under his carport until he could replace the windows. George said he could get them, and a radio, from a junkyard and do it himself. He would cover up the bullet hole in the trunk lid with an emblem or decal.

The next morning, I had him drive me back into Portsmouth and I borrowed Howell's old van for a few days. I let George drive my Studebaker until the Olds was fixed.

CHAPTER 37

George

GEORGE ARRIVED BACK AT THE MOTORCYCLE SHOP PROMPTLY AT 8:00 o'clock the following Tuesday morning. He was anxious to find out what he could do, and what the offer might be. Thomas led him into the back of the shop, which proved to be both roomy and cluttered. He opened a rear, overhead door and sunlight filled the room. There were nearly as many motorcycles back there as there were for sale in front. George noticed two of them appeared damaged from collisions and two others scraped up from falls.

Thomas said, "My mechanic was drafted a month ago and the work is piling up. His wife was my receptionist and bookkeeper. After he left, she went back to her family in North Carolina. Filling in for both of them in my spare time just doesn't cut it."

He led George to one of the smaller Harley's, a red and white Sprint, near the overhead door. "The engine is locked up on this one. The owner swears it happened just sitting in his yard, but I'm not buying that." He gestured toward a tool chest. "See what you can do with it by lunch time."

He pointed to a door on the side, "The Parts Department is over there and service manuals are on a rack inside." He went back up front, through the four-foot-wide pedestrian door, and left George alone.

George looked the bike over from top to bottom, getting it settled in his mind how everything worked. He found a manual and skimmed through it looking for clues. On his second pass going over the bike, he noticed something wrong. He looked around the shop for the items and tools he needed and while he was at it, he scanned the parts department. It wasn't hard to figure out the system, and his confidence was growing.

George returned to the motorcycle and went to work. Before long, he had the engine turning over with the kickstarter. Getting it to run proved to be a different matter though. He finally caught on that it possessed its own idiosyncrasies and he worked around that.

Less than two hours after Thomas left him alone with it, he was covered with sweat from stomping on the kickstarter, but he finally got it fired up. The roar filled the room and he was glad the big door was open. The door to the front half of the building flew open and Thomas came running through it. He raced to one side and flipped a switch. A large, squirrel-cage fan above the back door began drawing out the exhaust fumes.

"My God! You have it running. I thought the engine was froze up. What did you do?"

George was feeling proud. "It was a hydraulic lock. The owner left the gas turned on and it drained down through the carburetor and filled the engine. The float valve is probably leaking. I drained the gasoline out of the crankcase and changed the oil. I still couldn't get it started so I changed the spark plug. That did it."

"Where's the chain?"

"I took it off first. I didn't want the bike taking off without me and maybe leaving you with a new door."

Thomas laughed. "After it warms up, put the chain back on and take it for a test ride."

There was a half-acre lot behind the shop, and after some instruction from Thomas, George took his first ever motorcycle ride. It was akin to the first time he fired an M1. He was hooked.

Thomas was overjoyed and offered him a wage as high as one of the big-three dealers would have paid him. The owner of the Sprint didn't want it back, so George bought it himself.

CHAPTER 38

Will

I KNEW GEORGE STILL WANTED TO TEST ME. IT WAS OBVIOUS HE WAS suitably impressed with my handgun skills from the shootings in Virginia Beach. In his mind, I just didn't look tough enough when it came to fighting hand-to-hand.

Alphonse called us both earlier, excited about a gym he'd found in Norfolk. He said the building was in good condition but in a deteriorating neighborhood not far from the tunnel to Portsmouth.

George called me immediately after he got off the phone with Alphonse, wanting me to go see it with him. I had vacated the duplex in Craddock and planned to turn it back over to Mr. Howell so he could rent it out again. I liked the apartment and the neighborhood on Webster Avenue, and began moving into it after George left. After the move, I would initiate my option to buy it as an investment property. George was coming from Suffolk, so it was easy for him to pick me up along the way.

The gym was smaller than I expected, but was the lower half of a two-story building with four apartments on the upper floor. Inside, everything was brown or gray with accumulated smells from years of blood, sweat and tears. The smells blanketed a deeper, pissy odor in proximity to the shower and locker rooms.

The good news was that it held a boxing ring, wrestling mats and two-each, speed bags and heavy bags. Four rows of old-time wooden stadium seats on runners sat between the boxing and wrestling areas. Someone had remounted every other seat to face in the opposite direction, so each side had coverage. It was an odd arrangement, but I could see how it would work. A long, wooden table sat ahead of the front row on each side for judges. Years of dirty, sweaty hands gripping the seat arms and backs had blackened them in the areas not covered by shirts or sleeves.

On the wrestling side, mats on the corner walls rose above those on the floor. Alphonse was off examining the locker-shower area and I stepped over to the wrestling side to get a closer look at the blackened mats. George followed and when we were three feet from them, he shoved me hard from behind. "Go ahead, Hard Ass!"

I tripped on the edge of the mat and went down, but I was half-expecting something like that.

George pounced and I rolled. I wasn't able to get completely clear. He landed on my upraised elbow. It caught him in the solar plexus and knocked the wind out of him.

He rolled in the opposite direction, huffing and wheezing, but managed to get to a half-crouch before my shoe caught him in the left thigh. He gave out a grunt, but proved to be faster than I expected. He came up from his crouch and tried to head-butt me.

I moved my head to the side to avoid it just in time for a rock-hard fist to loosen a couple of teeth on the left side of my jaw and leave me dizzy. He wasn't done. He followed up with a left cross that I barely ducked under.

He was still swarming me when I caught him under the chin with a right uppercut that snapped his head back. I stood aside to let him fall, but he didn't. He wobbled but came right back with a flurry of punches.

I squatted, grabbed both of his legs, and heaved upward letting his momentum carry him on over my shoulder and down. This time, it was me pouncing on him. I dropped my ass on his chest and knocked the wind out of him again, then slapped his face for good measure. That really pissed him off.

He was strong and determined, but still wheezing, and we grappled around on the mat, both trying to gain advantage with different holds, knee strikes, kicks and punches. I gained top position again and he grabbed my shirt collar with one hand so he could punch me with the other.

I spit blood into his eyes and he turned his head away in surprise. I drove a fist down into his nose and saw his head bounce off the mat.

He threw me off with the strength of two men and for the first time we both were on our feet facing each other. He tried some sweeping kicks and some side kicks. They were fast and hard, but the karate stuff was right down my alley and I had a counter move for all of them.

We fought back and forth, up and down, for another ten minutes, both of us sucking wind. He was bigger and stronger, but I was a hair faster and more skilled. His fists felt like bricks, but I knew my kicks and karate chops did too. Finally, he managed to grab me and wrap his arms and legs around me like an octopus.

He anticipated my escape and countered it. Then he had my back from below. I was locked up tight and getting dizzy, with only one arm free.

I grabbed a finger and snapped it in the middle.

He let out a bellow and loosened his grip.

I rolled on top of him and drove an elbow into his ribs.

He tried to knee me in the groin but I rolled away, and kept rolling.

We both lay there on our backs, six feet apart.

"You broke my damn finger."

I rolled halfway over and spit a bloody molar at him. "You knocked out my tooth and I could have gouged out an eye. One of my hands was free."

We both started laughing. He knew I was right.

From the side, we heard applause. Alphonse and an older, white-haired colored man sat there in the stadium seats looking at us and clapping; both grinning like Cheshire cats.

When we managed to get to our feet, Alphonse said, "You boys are a sight. You was fightin' like two wildcats in a bag."

He introduced the other man as Doctor Mosher, the owner of the building. Doctor Mosher said, "Good thing I turned the water back on. You look like you've been painting barns, using one another for brushes."

The man turned out to be a fight doctor as well. After we showered and cleaned up as best we could, he splinted the little finger on George's left hand and told him to lie on his back while he straightened his nose. He used a speculum to open it up and then poked a small metal tube up each nostril and worked them around inside. Leaving them in place, he reshaped the outside with his thumb and forefinger.

While he was doing this, he said, "Between rounds during a boxing event, I would have gripped his nose between my thumb and forefinger and hammered the closed fist of my other hand down on top of them. It works, but not as well."

Afterward, he splinted and taped the nose before removing the tubes. I was pleased to see George wince from the pain and see his eyes water during the procedure.

Then it was my turn, but George had stitched me up not long before, so it was anticlimactic. The doctor turned to me and checked my jaw. "Your jaw's not broken and there's nothing I can do about the tooth. The others will tighten back up on their own. You need some stitches over your left eye though."

While that was going on, George looked at me and grinned a puffy grin. "You mind if I keep that tooth as a souvenir?"

As painful as it was, I laughed. "Keep it, I have the socket as a reminder. Next time we're in here, let's keep it civil, OK?"

"Don't worry, that was more than I needed. You're one tough piece of work, Will. I should have waited anyway, the wound in my side is killing me, too."

"I doubt that either of us will forget this one."

We shook and crossed thumbs in another grip—a bond of brothers.

Afterward, back in my apartment, I told him about some of the ways I could have hurt him worse. "I might have gouged out an eye or crushed your larynx. It's possible to drive a man's nose up into his brain and kill him. I could have kicked your healing liver or thigh, but I cut you some slack."

George was smart, he listened, so I continued. "In a street fight or in a building, look for anything you can use as a weapon, and almost anything can be used.

"Other than overextending joints, ignore the big bones. Go for the soft spots where there are major blood vessels or nerves. The little Filipino man sunk a key into his attacker's temple. Think past the rules. Rules are for sports.

"When you are fighting a man, look for his weaknesses. Look for what he tries to favor, what he needs to protect, and exploit it. Look for a tell in his eyes and in his body language."

We were standing, so I said, "Let me show you something."

"I'm all ears, Boss. This is good stuff."

I told him to grab my head or throat with both hands.

"I know this is going to hurt," he replied. He grabbed me behind the head with both hands and tried to pull my head down toward his chest.

I rammed the stiffened fingers of both hands up into his armpits, but not as hard as I could have. He let out a bellow as his arms flopped to the side out of control, and dropped. He collapsed to the floor and rolled onto his side, hugging his chest.

It took him a minute or two for him to get his breath back. "Son of a bitch, that hurt."

"Sorry, George. There are major nerves and blood vessels in the axilla. You will learn where others are over time."

As he regained his feet, he said, "Whoo! Well, I learned a new word for armpit too."

CHAPTER 39

George

GEORGE DROVE HIS TIRED, ACHING BODY BACK TO SUFFOLK. IT HAD been a grueling battle with Will, far worse than he expected. On the way back to the apartment in Portsmouth, Will told him of some of the other things he could have done to end the fight much sooner. He believed every word.

Will might well have gouged out an eye or broken an arm, or wrist. He might have used keys, or the buckle from his belt, or even items from George's pockets. He talked of Krav Maga, Silat fighting and Hapkido, three forms George never heard of before. Yet they seemed to be the deadliest. He vowed to learn all he could from Will. They would make good workout training partners, but wouldn't do so much personal damage to each other in the future.

Once he arrived back in Suffolk, he phoned Murta. "I can come yet today if you will have a room for me."

"Yes, come after 7:00 p.m. please. I will have a room for you."

"I've had a rough day. I might need some TLC."

"T L C?"

"Tender Loving Care. I'm bruised all over."

There was a pause... "I will give you tender, loving care all over. Call me when you are close to the hotel and I will tell you which room to go to."

Three hours later, George lay in a luxurious hotel bed with Murta gently massaging him and kissing his bruises. She gently eased on top of him, naked, and finished with a full body massage for both of them.

CHAPTER 40

Will

IT WAS A RELIEF TO BE ALONE IN THE APARTMENT, WHERE I COULD apply liniment and rest. No more than fifteen minutes after George left, I heard a commotion above me. First, it was a thumping, then grunts and squeals. They seemed to emanate from different rooms above me and included knocks on the floor above me as well. It didn't take a genius to figure out what was going on. George told me a young sailor's wife lived upstairs and the husband was out to sea. Maybe he was home.

It died down in about twenty minutes and I heard footsteps coming down the stairs. I looked out the front bedroom window to see what he looked like as he left, while I thought about Nina.

It was Steve Lewis.

* * *

The next day I called Nina. We talked for several minutes but she sensed something in my voice. "Will, are you eating something?"

"No, I have a toothache."

"Do you have medicine for it?"

"Yes." I lied.

She ignored what I said. "I will bring you some medicine and some soup. Where do you live?"

"Nina, OK, I have been in the gym, working out. There was an accident. I'm not in any kind of shape to see anyone right now."

There were a few seconds of silence—then, "What is your address?"

I gave in and told her. Afterward, I looked in the mirror. One side of my face was swollen and the eye on that side was nearly closed despite the icepack I'd put on it the night before. I had an inch-long cut over the end of the other eyebrow, with several black stitches.

Nina was no fool. As soon as she saw me, she knew I had been in a fight. It was hard to convince her it was a friendly fight. "If this was friendly, what happens if you fight and it is not friendly?" She seemed to delight in dabbing Merthiolate on my cut eyebrow and my skinned knuckles.

"I am a fighting instructor, Nina. Sometimes I am challenged by my students."

"The student beat you?"

"No, he looks much worse."

"Then there are two fools." There was no winning against her reasoning.

Despite the browbeating, she stayed the night with me. She hugged, kissed and cuddled with me, but we didn't get intimate. I lay awake half the night smelling the Ben-Gay that soaked through two of my T-shirts, one on me, one on her. Despite her body heat against me, her even breathing lulled me to sleep.

When I awoke in the morning, she was gone.

She left a note.

* * *

Dear Will,

You are a nice man, but a fighting man too. You cry out and fight in your sleep. You are some kind of soldier and I know you cannot resist that life or stay in one place.

I am very happy when I am with you. I care about you, but I fear you will be away from me more than you are with me. Some day you may not come back at all. I am so sorry, but I am not ready to commit to a life such as that.

Please do not call me.

Nina

* * *

I thought about the letter all day, and many times over during the years. I couldn't fault her for that. She was right. It saddened me even more that I hadn't been able to take her dancing. I hoped that someday, when I was ready to settle down, I would find another Nina. And I would be the man she wanted me to be.

My mind pondered the events of the past few weeks. I satisfied myself George and I and the others had done all we could regarding the Brazilian gang. I called the police with a fabricated story and a few more captives were rescued from the apartment Ji emerged from.

Murta and Marisol were safe and living a new life.

Many kidnapped men, women and children were now free.

The Howells were back in business with a lifetime income.

I found a lifelong friend in George Rickson and established a friendship with other men, men who I could count on to cover my back.

I also thought about what I had become.

Most important of all are the people I cry over in my sleep: those who, even if still alive, are too broken to ever be fixed. But for now, most of them were put to rest and I thought I would be able to relax for a while.

* * *

After I moved to Webster Avenue, I had Lavon's crew clean both of the Craddock units so I could turn the building back over to Mr. Howell. If Nina ever changed her mind and came back, she would go to Webster Avenue anyway.

CHAPTER 41

ON A WARM, EARLY NOVEMBER AFTERNOON, AS I RETURNED TO THE apartment from a brief shopping trip, I noticed an unfamiliar car with Florida license plates. The area was populated with transients from Portsmouth Naval Hospital, and it was parked around the corner from the house, so I didn't think too much about it. There was a man sitting in it on the passenger side, but he never glanced up as I drove by.

Cars filled all of the parking spaces in front of my house, so I circled the block and parked across the street. As I stepped out, I noticed a woman sitting on my porch steps. My first thought was that it was my upstairs neighbor, but then I realized it wasn't her. Nina flashed through my mind, but I knew it wasn't her either. It was someone familiar, though.

Forgetting about my groceries and everything else, I was nearly run over by a passing pickup truck as I started across the street.

The woman held a baby swaddled in her arms, and all of a sudden I knew who she was.

"Eva!" I gasped.

She rose and stepped down onto the sidewalk so we were face-to-face. I noticed her magnificent body—a body I remembered so well—was covered from neck to toe. She wore a light, tan coat over a brown turtleneck sweater. Below the coat were black slacks and black pumps.

She looked me straight in the eye. "Hello Will."

"What are you doing here, Eva? And who is this little fellow?"

"This is John, and I needed to talk to you, so I tracked you down."

"How did you do that?"

"I met a man named Jerry Smith, a veteran. He knows you and he helped me."

"Come on inside, Eva."

"No, I can't go inside."

While she was talking, I was looking at the baby. He just smiled up at me. Gears jammed in my brain as I tried to imagine what was going on. This little guy had light brown hair, blue eyes and my oval-shaped face. I just couldn't get it to add up.

"John who?" I asked.

"John Lutz. He was born April 15th and he is seven months old." She paused, and then continued, "His name might have been John Real-Bad. Sit down Will, and I'll tell you about it."

I had to sit down. My knees were shaking.

Eva sat too, but on the step below mine.

"Will, my husband wasn't dead. It was a mistaken identity. He suffered massive injuries and lost an arm and a leg. He may never fully recover, but he is still the man I love and he still loves me. His name is Tony.

"I found out about Tony only two weeks after you left, but he didn't get home from overseas for another three months. He was with me when John was born and he loves him as much as I do. John is the only child we will ever have."

I gripped my hands between my knees to keep from reaching out to her and the baby. My head was spinning.

"What can I do?" I just couldn't picture myself as a father, especially a traditional father. Yet, I wanted them both.

We were just far enough apart that we were not touching. She glanced down at the baby and back up at me.

"Will, Tony and I believe it's only fair you know you are a father. That's why I'm here. However, John is our son, both legally and in our hearts. It would be too hard on Tony for you to be around us. I am asking you. Please stay away from Ocala. We want nothing else from you, but I will be happy to let you know how John is doing at least once a year."

I started to speak, I had a hundred questions, but she held up a hand up to stop me.

She said, "John will be told of your paternity when he is old enough—probably eighteen."

"OK, but how will I ever see him?"

I saw her visibly relax at my words. I wanted to know what Tony was capable of as a provider? What kind of income he would have? What would be their standard of living? I wanted to know how I would see John, and so much more?

Eva tensed up again. "I can't let you see him in person. He already looks too much like you, and he would figure it out way too soon… Tony doesn't know that."

Now I tensed up again. "But how?"

"I will send you pictures or films, when we can make them."

I leaned back and propped my elbows on the step behind me, thinking things over while she fussed over little John, my son who has my great, great grandfather's name. Finally, I said, "I would like to help financially."

"Help will be appreciated, whatever you can do, but you are under no obligation."

"Yes, I am. If not for you, most certainly for him. I will send money orders so you can cash them wherever you wish."

I would do a whole lot more, but right then wasn't the time to tell her. I thought about giving her my fist two fifties, the ones I had hidden in the house, but I had second thoughts about that. It was blood money and I didn't want to hand her that. Instead, I decided to start a trust fund for John with them. I said, "If you don't have a post office box, get one and send me the address. If you have something to write on, I'll give you my PO box number."

While she was digging in her bag, I reached over to have a better look at John Lutz. He gazed back at me as solemnly as a Chinese monk. His skin was mine-with-a-tan, eyes, ears and nose were all mine. He had only Eva's complexion. There was no doubt this was my son.

While she was writing down the address I gave her, I leaned over and kissed him on the forehead. He never made a sound, just kept looking at me. I had to move back from his gaze.

Eva stood up with her bundle and said, "Goodbye Will. I wish you the best." She touched me lightly on the arm; just the way she did the first time she came to my uncle's house. Then she turned and quickly walked away with John—around the corner to that waiting car with Florida plates.

EPILOGUE

I MOVE AROUND THE COUNTRY AS THE SEASONS AND MY INCLINA-
tions direct me. It's not hard to pick up a newspaper or watch the news
on television. There's always a sleaze out there somewhere, running
around loose after doing great bodily harm, or worse, to a rich man's
loved ones.

Regardless of religious or political affiliations, rich men are
good for business, Real-Bad business. Sometimes they aren't rich and
there is no financial reward. And that's all right too, as long as justice
is served.

Sometimes, depending on circumstances, I go by William Real,
William Battle, W. E. Battle or Will Battle——a name hung on me by
Robert Cee after my fight with the Turks in Stuttgart.

Occasionally, I call upon George, Robert Cee, Steve Lewis,
Alphonse, Sonny Metz or others like them for help—help that is
almost a reward in itself. Sometimes I need protection for myself too.
Evil springs up like mushrooms and others will keep coming for me.
My calling guarantees it.

End

Many thanks to my Editor, Dave Grimmett, and to those who proofread and supplied moral support:

Janie Broadhead

Author Frank Allan Rogers

Mary Schillo

Veda M. Smith

Jerry Smith US Army Ret. RIP

BadBob Johnson USMC Ret. RIP

Dave Norem has ridden alone over most of the Continental US on a motorcycle, walked alone in strange cities at night - in ethnic areas of large cities - in forests at night - and in foreign lands... always wondering what lay ahead, over the next hill or around the next bend. His short stories have been published in magazines and anthologies.

* * *

Other books by Dave Norem

RECURRENCE

PAPERTOWN